M|

If Ethan Clay Should Hang

A convicted killer, a governor teetering on the edge of political oblivion and an outlaw territory on the brink of chaos. All were broiling beneath a murderous August sun.

Nobody wanted the job of escorting local hero Ethan Clay from his home county across the desert for his date with death on the governor's gallows. Then, along came Charron. Iron man Charron quickly showed that neither assassins nor ambushers could prevent him reaching Capital City with his prisoner safely in chains.

As the friends of Ethan Clay rose up in violent protest, outlaw territory learned two things: the young killer was a far greater threat than the governor had realized and, secondly, big Ben Charron was a true gladiator of the gun. Much lead would fly before these lessons were learnt.

If Ethan Clay Should Hang

Paul Wheelahan

A Black Horse Western

ROBERT HALE · LONDON

ISBN 0 7090 7222 8

Robert Hale Limited
Clerkenwell House
Clerkenwell Green
London EC1R 0HT

Typeset by
Derek Doyle & Associates, Liverpool.
Printed and bound in Great Britain by
Antony Rowe Limited, Wiltshire

CHAPTER 1

THE DESERT RIDER

The casa of José Morelos gleamed whitely behind the deep green of the hardy bougainvillaea that had triumphed over the west wall of the adobe and now encroached upon the portico itself.

Sam Jackson sat drowsing on the stoop in the heat blowing in off the desert. The hawk-faced gunman was dreaming of the old days before he'd become a manhunter, of the paynight blowout with young men of his own low station – when a man could sleep nights without a gun under his pillow, to dream of a good woman waiting for him someplace and maybe someday a child of his own to give him some humble immortality . . .

He stirred and smiled his cruel cat smile, scornful of

5

what he'd once been. Gone were those days, and he didn't miss them a bit.

A heavy oak table stood on the worn porchboards directly behind the man. Upon it rested a bottle of tequila, a glass, a Colt .45.

Harlan Jenner sat at the table with long legs crossed. He wore a full-sleeved white silk shirt opened at the throat. The light bouncing off the adobe's whitewashed walls glinted off the taut bronze of his cheekbones and sheened his high-brushed black hair. He sat motionless with a long black cigarillo burning away in the fastest right hand in Tolorosa County.

'He's way overdue,' Jackson grunted.

'I know it.'

'Mebbe he took the Two Springs trail down from the canyon instead instead of this 'un.'

'Two waterholes that route, five this one.' Jenner inclined his sleek head toward the faint trace of trail winding in off the malpais. 'Which one would you take?'

'Neither. Only an idjut'd cross this desert in August.'

Jenner tapped ash from his stogie and squinted into the painful glare. 'He's crossing it,' he murmured. He sounded sure. Then he nodded with a frown. 'But you could be right about this geezer. If he doesn't show in an hour it could mean he's coming out by way of Two Springs and Coyoteville.'

'We head there then?'

'What do you think?'

Silence fell. They went back to smoking and waiting for the first sign of a horseman emerging from the brutal glare of the desert. A big bronzed man with rain-coloured eyes and a reputation.

Waiting to kill.

Ben Charron strode out of the burning desert leading eighteen hands of sore-footed grulla by a lead rope which his horse had chewed halfway through. He had been burning up boot leather ever since noon when the last leg of the desert crossing finally took its toll on his mount. He had no time for a quitter, whether it travelled by two legs or four, but the reality was that the fifteen-mile stretch they'd just put behind them would test the mettle of a camel. But they'd made it, which was all that counted, and soon through the haze he could make out the blue-green tones of the low hills, and he heard what sounded like women's voices coming to him on the burning air of the late afternoon.

He stopped to shake his head, rivulets of sweat cutting tracks down through the alkali dust coating his cheeks. By his calculations Coyoteville was still a couple of miles distant. And even if the town was closer, who would be laughing and singing on a day when you'd swear they'd left open the furnace gates of Hell?

The horse, played-out, parched and in mean temper, attempted to savage Ben's arm. Almost absently, Charron rapped its teeth with a hard elbow. He jerked on the rope and attacked the shaley slope leading up to the landmark pile of Monument Rocks which afforded a sweeping panorama of the arid rangelands, where he realized his hearing hadn't been playing him tricks after all.

He blinked slowly.

Some half mile directly ahead where the lower Red Creek traced its shallow course along the fringe of the desert down from Coyoteville, pretty girls were dancing in the water.

They were supposed to be working this time of day. The washerwomen were paid by the number of baskets of clothing they beat clean on sunwashed stones, not for disporting their ripe young bodies under a slanting sun.

But the day had been long and hot, the grim *señora* who presided over their labours had returned to town – and they were young and the water was sparkling and there was nobody to spy on them out here, so why not?

Yet even though it was strictly forbidden for menfolk to wander down here while the girls and young women of Coyoteville were at their chores, a wary eye was still kept on the eastern bluffs just in case, men being what they were.

Nobody was concerned about the wide western aspect where the faint trace of a little-used trail wound out of the desert. Even *bandidos*, lawmen and lonesome wanderers avoided the desert May to October.

Mostly, that was.

Charron bit off the tip of a short black Dollar cigar and set it alight with the sweep of a lucifer. He coughed. His throat felt like sandpaper. Ever since they'd hit the malpais he'd been feeding the horse from his own water canteen to keep it going, with the result he was thirstier than Carrie Nation in Whiskey City.

Flicking the dead match away, he started down from

the cluster of pale blue boulders for the creek, with the westering sun at his back, and he covered half the distance to the water unobserved. His expression didn't alter as the women drew nearer and he saw the way afternoon light shimmered off bouncing breasts and dancing thighs barely concealed by skimpy underclothing. Yet he didn't watch for long, his wary gaze quickly drifting away from all this lush Spanish beauty to the low sandstone river ridges and the cluster of rooftops beyond the distant bridge. He was a man on a dangerous assignment now entering a region where every man or woman could prove a deadly enemy.

He covered another fifty yards before the cry went up: '*Gringo! Arriba, arriba!*'

By now he was within spitting distance of the creek. He paused and lifted a big right hand, palm forward in the universal sign of peace, but only the tallest girl, the one with hair trailing waist-length and flimsy petticoat tucked up into her knickers, stood her ground as her companions rushed for their dresses.

She eyed him wrathfully, hands on hips and dark eyes glittering dangerously.

'*Perverso!*' she accused belligerently. Then, '*Cuisado!* Leave us, *gringo*, or by the Virgin—'

'Relax,' he growled, stepping down stiffly. He had a thirst like a rat eating red pepper. Hunkering at the water's edge, he pushed his hat back and began drinking from cupped hands, the grulla sinking its dusty muzzle luxuriously several feet downstream.

The girl didn't relax but appeared to lose some of

9

her indignation as she studied him at close quarters. She saw how big and broad he was, with spatulate fingers and the shoulders of a day laborer. He was dressed in varying shades of brown; dark-brown hat dusted in alkali, bronzed shirt, tan pants, yellow-hued gunrig and boots.

His .45 was worn low and thonged to the thigh in a fashion not lost on the girl and her gaping companions. But only a big bold girl like this would dare ask, '*Pistolero?*'

Charron straightened and stretched his aching body, arching his back. He was staring off towards the town and either hadn't heard or didn't mean to answer. In that long moment's silence, the women and girls were able to assess him more calmly.

They found him impressive if anything but reassuring, and quickly the realization hit that this was indeed no field hand, despite the powerful physique; they sensed indeed that Angelique was most likely right about him.

Such men were no strangers to Rosanna Valley. Down here in the borderlands such riders came and went with monotonous regularity these days in a period where the old, cruel aristocratic reign of the Spanish overlords was being seriously challenged by the surging tide of American expansion. Drifters, adventurers, soldiers of fortune and outlaws on the run – Rosanna County saw them all come and go, and poor *paisano* women like them had learned to avoid them wherever possible, or treat them with wary respect when contact proved unavoidable.

But there were always people who just couldn't seem to accept the notion that big *gringos* with heavy guns were the new lords of creation. Angelique was one, and her black eyes suddenly sharpened with a new suspicion as he began to lead the horse across the creek; *their* creek.

'*Uno momento, Señor Pistolero*,' she said accusingly.

He halted, looked back over his shoulder. 'What?'

She gestured.

'You come in from the desert which no man travels in this season. You wear your pistol low, and you have the look . . .'

'What look would that be?'

'The look of the wolf.'

He scowled, but she met his gaze defiantly. A big-breasted, healthy young female animal, she stood like a Spanish warrior princess with her golden columnar legs apart and water lapping dimpled knees.

A sneer flicked the edges of his mind. Before too long this one would be presiding over a run down adobe hovel with a husband too proud to work and a gaggle of dark-eyed kids to feed, he brooded. Looking forty before she reached thirty. Why should he listen to her? What was her opinion worth?

A blousy young woman with a flower in her hair said anxiously, 'Angelique, you must not offend the *señor*.'

'That's OK,' Charron grunted, adjusting the set of his bedroll. 'I'm not the sensitive breed.'

Angelique drew a step closer. 'Then, just what breed

11

are you, *gringo*? Not *vaquero*, miner, drummer or merchant, of this I am sure. You have rifle, *pistola* ... and boxes of bullets in your saddle-bags, I am sure. Do you know who and what I think you are?'

The sun was dropping fast. He had a footsore horse, and needed brandy and a three-course meal in a hurry. She was irritating him, yet she also provoked his curiosity.

'Who?'

Her lovely face twisted with contempt.

'You are the one who has come for Ethan Clay in Rio Salto, are you not? Our great governor's evil gunman whom he has sent to drag an innocent *hombre* back to Capital City and the executioner in his black hood. We have been waiting for you, *Señor* Charron, and now like a slinking cur you have come. No?'

Charron tilted his hat to conceal his reaction.

They knew! They even knew his name.

The job of work that had brought him from the capital to Rosanna County was intended to be a closely guarded secret. Plainly it was nothing of the kind. If a simple washerwoman knew about it, then the whole damned territory had to know!

Without a word he led the horse through the water where it trickled over cool pale stones.

'*Asesino!*'

He continued on until he reached the bank. He turned and looked back.

'You're wrong,' he said. 'I'm no more an assassin than Ethan Clay's an innocent man.' He swung up and settled into the saddle. 'Not that it matters a damn, but where'd you hear that tall tale anyhow?'

'You deny it is so?'

'Maybe.'

'Then that makes you both a liar and a killer!'

She turned her head and spat into the water. An older woman waded to her side and seized her by the arm, urging restraint. When they looked up, the man was in his saddle and riding away.

'Look at him run!' the girl snorted contemptuously. Then, astonishingly, her whole attitude seemed to change in an instant. She clapped a hand over her heart and looked comically tragic. 'Ah, but Mother of the Holy Virgin of Guadaloupe, will you just look at those shoulders!'

The others began to smile. Angelique had enjoyed her moment of drama, but it had all been pure theatrics. None of them cared a plug damn about wild man Ethan Clay. They held no loyalties for any American desperado, any more than they really cared who might take him away or who hang him. They were too concerned with simple survival to worry about such things, and with a half hour of daylight still left, they soon happily returned to their work and the big *gringo* was soon forgotten. Such ones came and went, but the work was always with them.

Charron reached the outskirts of the town afoot, leading the limping grulla. He walked slowly, dust-coated boots dragging a little in the dirt. Ahead in the dusk he could see where the rutted road opened into an untidy plaza with the bell tower of a tiny church rising above a row of adobes flanked by the unpainted plank and batten buildings of the new time.

He made his way to a livery and left the horse to be groomed, watered and fed, making certain the big-nosed liveryman understood exactly what was expected of him.

By now the scattered streetlamps were fluttering yellow flames, casting a warm glow that softened the hard edges of reality.

Hat tilted back, he halted beneath a light pole to tug a stubby black Dollar cheroot from his breast pocket. He set it between his teeth and scraped a Vesta into life upon the pole. The quick flare of the match revealed the dark gleam of his eyes flickering over storefronts, barns, stables and saloons. He drew smoke deep and flicked the dead match away. Coyoteville was much as he expected – the sleepy Mexican past blending uneasily with the new time. Most of the people he saw were Mexican, but his gaze picked out the odd American travelling the rickety plankwalks between the cantinas.

He fingered a speck of tobacco from the tip of his tongue and grimaced.

His anger at the realization that his job was no longer secret had quickly passed. He was dealing with the reality of this now. He'd left the Capital three days earlier, deliberately taking the hostile desert route to save time and avoid attracting attention. It seemed all too plain now that the news that Governor Lane had dispatched a troubleshooter to escort a convicted killer back north must have immediately gone humming along the telegraph now linking either side of the desert to the south, for the information to have spread so quickly.

What sort of top level security was that?

The Clay assignment had looked challenging enough for him as it stood without anybody and everybody with a vested interest in trying to save the killer's hide being tipped off about it.

But what if nobody really cared? he had to ask himself.

What if all the speculation round the county capital that painted a picture of the renegades down here banding together to rally round the killer and install him as some kind of figurehead in their ongoing conflict with the north proved to be just so much hot air and newspaper gossip?

How could a man find out?

He could start by taking a good look around, that's what he could do.

Coyoteville was familiar enough to someone who'd spent almost as much time in recent years south of the border as above; poverty-stricken, squalid, dismal and bleak. He took a walk, found nothing unusual, yet still wasn't reassured. Either he was more played-out from his forced trek across the barren lands than he figured, or else there was something about this pesthole that just didn't sit right.

He was not a trusting man, but he trusted his instincts.

15

Back on the plaza he visited the liveries in turn, checking out the stalls, asking questions about any new arrivals. He was met by blank faces and shrugging shoulders. They acted like they didn't really understand what he was about. Maybe they were on the level. Maybe.

He registered at the town's only hotel. His room overlooked a small walled yard where an enormous yellow cat prowled amongst potted cacti. A slatternly housemaid enquired whether he had any other gear than the saddle-bags he carried over one shoulder. He slung her a silver dollar and told her his name. She yawned and scratched an armpit, shaking her head languidly, yet studying him intently from under hooded eyelids all the same.

With him appearing to fill the small room as he stood before her, with hands resting on shellbelt and lamplight sheening his broad brown face, the woman was thinking idly how he seemed big and powerful enough not really to need that big, walnut-butted gun riding his thigh. But, of course, in these troubled times, all men wore guns, just as they wore hats to protect them from the sun.

And she did recognize his name, even though she insisted otherwise. Charron was certain of this and could no longer deny he smelt trouble in the evening air as he mentally said goodbye to his plan to strip off, stretch out and grab that twelve hours' sleep he desperately needed.

Men in his line of work who ignored the promptings

16

of their sixth sense rarely got to be old men.

He'd been fully briefed before quitting Governor Matherson Lane's plush office. Clay was the son of a Territorian beauty and a border rebel. His reputation as a horseman and hellraiser had seen him attract wide local sympathy when the rumour spread that he'd been railroaded on a murder charge.

Such a factor was enough to make any loser respectable down here in outlaw territory where most men were 'agin' the government' anyway, and where Clay's mix of credentials was sufficient to make him some kind of shoddy hero.

There were powerful elements committed to the downfall of the incumbent administration in the upcoming elections and these were stridently critical of Lane's somewhat obvious political decision to hang Clay in the Capital in order to focus maximum attention upon the 'success' of his highly touted war against the lawbreakers in this rebellious corner of his political kingdom.

So great was the interest in the Clay affair that Charron found it easy enough to believe that someone might try and stop him doing his job. If they had the stones for it.

It was a quiet night at the cantina.

The barkeep with the enormous drum-gut, into which he poured an unending cascade of tepid beer every single night during his fourteen-hour stints, was yarning with a sheepman from the hills and two wranglers from vast Anvil Ranch up from the south. A

17

weary percenter was trying to interest the bunch of card players seated about a circular table, beneath a dense cloud of tobacco smoke, in her only-average charms, but the stakes were high, the tequila passable and, for once, a genuinely interesting topic of conversation had them engrossed, so it seemed she was destined to be out of luck.

The bum in the broken hat was first to pick out the towering figure who appeared with hands resting on the tops of the batwings for a long moment before entering.

Every head turned.

The Yanqui's size alone was enough to attract attention, yet it was his eyes, rain-coloured and hard, that held it.

Then the men shrugged. They had seen such strangers before and mostly what they did or who they were proved of little consequence to Coyoteville.

He crossed to the bar where the vast bartender put on his mine host's welcoming smile.

'Whiskey, *señor*?'

'Brandy.' The saddle-bags hit the counter with a thud. 'Clean glass.'

By the time his order was filled the cantina showed some signs of relaxing. But Charron kept alert, feeling their eyes upon him as he drained his glass. Both mine host and the cowboys seemed to be watching him too closely as he unbuckled a saddle-bag and drew from it a small, heavy moneysack of soft doeskin. Wordlessly he drew the tie and upended the sack to dump a dozen

18

little yellow nuggets on the bartop.

Nobody was even pretending not to be watching him now. He had their undivided attention.

'My name's Charron and I've come south to collect a piece of trash named Ethan Clay for the county hangman,' he announced roughly, eyes playing over the sea of faces. 'If that means there could be men hereabouts looking to stop me doing my job, I need to know about it. Savvy?'

He paused to pick up four nuggets, one by one, and dropped them into the palm of his left hand. You could hear the quiet.

'The price of four blood horses is the going fee for what I need to know . . . and you can all figure out what that is. I'll be at the hotel.'

He left without another word. On the porch he waited until he heard the buzz of conversation break out, then he headed away across the dusty little square. Times like this you never appealed to patriotism, decency or a sense of fair play to get what you were after; you just showed them the money.

10.30.

Stripped to the waist with a watered brandy in his fist, Charron rose from the straw-bottomed chair and moved about his darkened room. Without showing himself at the window he gazed out over the moon-washed yard.

Two hours.

Either the bait wasn't working or Coyoteville had

nothing to tell him. He refused to believe the latter. Weary beyond belief now, he was still razor-sharp and alert, knew he would remain so until first light if nobody took his bait. If daylight came without incident, he would set out for the south on a lame horse and admit his instincts had played him false . . .

He swung his head at the sounds of a disturbance in the corridor outside. He heard a scuffling sound, a woman's drunken voice, followed by a hard slapping sound.

'Leave go of me, damn you!' a slurred voice protested. 'It's a free country and I can tell that dirty hired gun what I think of him and nobody's got the right to stop me—'

The voice broke off as Charron opened his door and stepped into the passageway. The blousy woman with the bottle stopped struggling in the grip of the hostelero, red-rimmed eyes blazing.

'Just what I expected!' she said scornfully. 'They call it law and order they dole out up at the Capital, yet they hire cheap gunslingers to do their dirty work for them!' She shook a heavily ringed finger. 'That feller you wanna hang is innocent as a jaybird, Charcoal, or whatever they call you. And if you haul him back to the hangman you'll have a murder on your soul – if you've got one. You hear me, you big hog-butcher? Murderer!'

At that point a man appeared hurriedly with a flustered apology. The drunk was hustled away, still waving her bottle and yelling abuse.

Partially opened doors whispered closed again as

the racket faded. Charron re-entered his room, saw the face at his window and dropped to one knee, palming the big black Colt.

'No, *señor*!' the scrawny paisano gasped, eyes bugging in terror. '*Por favor*, I have come to tell you that which you would know.'

Still holding the gun, Charron rose and booted the door shut before crossing to the window. Reaching out, he took purchase on a soiled white shirt and hauled the lightweight bodily into the room. His nose crinkled. The man smelt like a charnel house.

'What?' he growled, the gun muzzle touching a stubbled chin. 'You'd better make it good, *hombre*.'

Two of them, he was told. Two tall Yanqui gunmen had come to town sometime after nightfall in search of Señor Charron, the *'gobernador's'* man. The bum claimed they were waiting at the livery until Charron slept before coming after him. And now that he knew, could he please pay him his gold in order that he might fork his burro and ride for the desert before the town found out he had turned traitor?

Charron interrogated the man for several minutes until reasonably convinced he could be speaking the truth. You could never be totally certain about anything in his line of work; you learned to go with percentages. He paid the fellow off, bundled him out through the window, then went to his saddle-bags. He was wearing two Colts with a heavy extra shellbelt slung over his shoulder as he crossed the hotel's moon-shadowed rear yard to make his way south for the livery.

21

CHAPTER 2

LAST MAN STANDING

The side door of the livery creaked open and the soft chiming of spurs heralded the return of Harlan Jenner before his tall figure appeared in the dimness.

'What?'

Jackson's voice was taut. He was a man of action who hated waiting.

'What – nothing. His horse is still here, he's still there, and time is on our side. You're not getting jittery on me, are you?'

Resentment darkened Jackson's broad face as he hauled a .45 to check the loads. He started at a small sound. 'What was that?'

'Maybe he's out there,' Jenner taunted. 'Big bad Charron manhandling a Gatling across to the forge

22

where he can set it up then trigger this whole damn building into sawdust. Want to go take a look, pard?'

'Damn you, Harlan—!' Jackson began, jumping up, but bit off his words when the other held up a placating hand.

'OK, OK, I was only fooling.' Jenner nodded emphatically. 'Right, I say we've waited long enough for Charron to nod off. Time to ride.'

'We're riding round to the hotel? Half a block?'

'Why did you think I kept our prads saddled?' Jenner replied, turning to go. 'Sure we're riding. Charron's room overlooks the yard. We're going to ride straight to his window and open up with all we've got. We'll hit so fast he won't even wake before he's with his Maker.' He tapped his forehead with a forefinger, careful not to disturb his perfect hair. 'I've been checking the hotel layout and doing the figuring while you've been playing with your cutters . . .' He broke off as the other man frowned. 'What now?'

Jackson shrugged.

'Well, it's just that I figured that when we caught up with Charron you'd, like, wanna call him out personal. You know? Duel him man to man?'

'You wouldn't be hinting that I don't have the sand to do that, would you, boy?'

'Hell no, Harl, I just thought . . . Jeez, who cares what I thought? We're bein' paid big dough to get the bum, so let's go earn it, eh?'

Jenner didn't speak as they mounted in the gloom and eased their rested horses out into the yard. He was

23

angry. Vanity was his Achilles. He'd duel anything on two legs. But this was business. He was about to speak when a low voice reached them from the shadowed bulk of the feed and grain barn opposite.

'Looking for me, scum?'

The gunmen jerked to a halt, off balance. But Jenner recovered in an instant. His blurring right hand filled with a sixgun as he demonstrated the clean draw that had made him famous. In the same instant, Jackson jerked his horse round in a half circle to get a clear line of fire. The animal's hindquarters crashed into Jenner's mount, ruining his aim. His bullet hammered harmlessly into the hayloft above Charron's dim outline in the same instant that the big man's guns crashed in deafening unison.

Jackson groaned faintly and began to slide from his saddle. Jenner ducked low as hot lead scorched across his shoulders. He raked brutally with his spurs and went rocketing for the far corner of the barn in a zigzagging run that saw him evade the searching lead.

A moment later he was safe and Charron blinked from sight.

The ferocious echo of the guns resounded like a gong beaten in the empty street, drowning the hammer of hoofs and the thud of running boots as Charron pounded down the alleyway for the square.

When he burst into the open, there was no sign of Jenner. Chest heaving, jaw muscles working, he hauled up to reload. He eased back into a doorway watching lights appear in the windows, his eyes filled with

24

sallow fire, a crouched savagery there.

Soon he heard loud voices in the next street coming from the direction of the cantina. He legged it in that direction, running hard. He put the length of a twisting alley behind him to bring the cantina into sight, slid to a halt in the shadows. The tall gunman was there on his long-legged pinto, haranguing a knot of men crowding the sagging porch.

'A fifty-dollar gold piece for every man who helps me get this bastard!' Jenner bawled, struggling to keep his nervy horse steady. 'Come on, who's with me, boys?' The mob's reaction was mixed, with several starting down the steps to join Jenner, but most others holding back. Charron didn't give them time to get organized. He'd recognized Harlan Jenner, and you never gave this breed a second chance to do you in.

He spread his legs, big head taut on flaring shoulders, his breath running in and out in slow gusts as he raised both guns.

'Jenner! Here!'

His voice was rifle-shot loud. Jenner's head jerked and the gun in his right hand exploded, the sound of the shot swallowing the echoes of the shout. Charron felt the hot airwhip of the slug's passage when it whipped by his neck. His shoulders rolled as he jerked twin triggers to smash Jenner from his saddle where he became a blur beneath his stamping horse. Yet the gunman instantly triggered from the ground, and angry towners chimed in to rake the storefront with a brutal hailstorm of fire.

25

But Charron was gone. He'd done what he'd had to do here, but his real job was still waiting down south. They heard the slow thud of his hoofbeats as he crossed the plank bridge out of town some time later, as they struggled to sober up the town vet to try and dig no less than three .45 slugs out of Jenner's fine hide.

First blood to the governor's man.

'What's he want for breakfast today?'

'Who?'

'Who do you think? Him. The goddamn prisoner.'

'Well, somethin' mighty sweet, I figure. Just loves his sugar, that young butcher does.'

'Butcher? Thought you claimed he never done it?'

'Well, guess I did. But now nigh everyone is agreein' it must've been Clay what blew Ricardo Valdez into Hades, ever since that Capital City judge found him guilty. The governor sure believes it, even if the sheriff don't. Why else would he go to all that trouble of shiftin' the execution from here to the Capital?'

'Why else?' growled the senior deputy. 'Politics is why else. Lane figures hangin' the kid up there'll get him re-elected.' The junior deputy looked confused.

'So, mebbe that's how it is, mebbe it ain't. What I don't unnerstand is, seein's as how Clay's about the biggest news in the territory right now, and with all this hoopla about his wild boys and other folks who admire him plottin' to bust him out, how come Lane never sent a whole squad of cavalry down to fetch him, or at least a posse of deputies? How dumb is it,

26

givin' a job that size to one gunhawk?'

'Son,' the older badgetoter sighed, getting up, 'like I said, it's all political.'

'How could assignin' a hired gun to do law work be political, consarn it?'

'The law and order issue is what you got to understand. The governor's been lookin' shakier and shakier on that score all year, and you can wager me the governor figures by sendin' a big bunch down here to get one flash killer he'd be acknowledgin' to the world that he'd let things get out of hand. So, instead he sends just one man. Foxy, boy. Smart play.'

His youthful brow furrowed in his struggle to grasp the duplicity and intrigue of matters political, the younger man was about to reply when the soulful strains of a harmonica drifted in from the cells.

'That means he wants to eat now,' he muttered. He glanced at the window. 'Look at that. False dawn just breakin'. Who eats at this time of day, for Pete's sake?'

'The kid is who. Oh yeah, and the sheriff. Better get the pot on the stove for the boss's coffee, you know how downright testy the boss's been ever since we got word about Charron.'

'And just how do you figure that information leaked out anyways, Joe?'

'Fix the joe. I can sense the sheriff on his way and I jest sense he's gonna be touchier even than a teased snake this mornin'.'

The deputy knew his superior well. The sheriff of Rio Salto was both abroad and in testy temper as his

27

tall lean figure made its slow way, still more asleep than awake, toward the jailhouse-courtroom building from his five-room adobe on Cardeas Avenue. He came trudging along the echoing planks of the sidewalk bordering the north side of the empty square like a sleepwalker as first light came to Rio Salto with a pale lemon haze in the eastern sky.

Humphrey Reed's custom was to work late and sleep in the mornings, but all that had changed since Ethan Clay gunned down one of the county's leading citizens.

Now nothing would be the same in Rio Salto until the convicted Red Creek hellion was gone to meet his Maker on the governor's gallows. The deputies had better have the coffee on when he reached the jailhouse, he thought sourly. Then he nodded to himself. Of course they would have brewed up by this time; their prisoner would see to that. Must be some hoot owl in Clay's bloodlines someplace, the hours he kept.

Mostly, early mornings here were quiet, but today was different, with plenty of citizens to be seen gathered about in dark knots, talking and gesticulating and showing their nervousness. Lights showed at the livery, stage depot and telegraph office as well as over at the jailhouse and courthouse spread which occupied most of the south side of the square.

By contrast with the surrounding buildings, the telegraph office was mint-new and garishly painted. The telegraph was the big new thing in this sprawling borderland town. The technological marvel of the decade had spanned the continent well before this, but had only recently managed to string its gaunt poles the long way round the vast tract of the intervening desert which had isolated Rosanna County from the more progressive northlands for so long. The keys in the little office had been chattering all night long, bringing reports on the violent events up in Coyoteville which had kept half the town awake until daybreak and beyond.

One man killed, another badly shot, and the Governor's man on his way; so ran the grim bulletins. Small wonder folks didn't sleep good any more.

Reed was finally beginning to come fully awake by the time he crossed a side street, where he paused to light his first cigarette of the day. He frowned. As if things hadn't been bad enough, what with the Valdez killing and Clay's arrest. Now there'd been last night's murderous gun battle up in Coyoteville to bring the pot to the boil. Despite Reed's protests, the governor's gunman had shown up and had already killed one man and seriously wounded another even before reaching Rio Salto.

Why wasn't he surprised?

Was it any wonder a man felt like starting the day with a double at the cantina?

'Any sign of him, Sheriff?'

The sheriff blinked back to the present to find the town's gunsmith standing before him in the strengthening light. The man, normally a stolid type of citizen, today appeared jittery and excited.

'Who?' Reed could be curt when it suited. 'What the devil are you talking about, man?'

'The shootist from the Capital, of course, Sheriff.

29

Charron. Guess he'll be somethin' to see, huh?'

'Get the hell out of my sight before I arrest you for talking like a damn fool, Wilson. Go on – get!'

The gunsmith had never seen him so testy. He scooted off, glancing back fearfully over his shoulder as he headed for the stage depot where he would be first to warn the early shift that their sheriff was coming apart at the seams.

Shaking his head disgustedly, Reed turned to squint at the crescent of the sun just emerging from the jagged teeth of the Hotspurs before continuing on his way. He paused to peer through the windows of the early opening tortilla joint, then craned his neck to glance up at the upper balcony of Rosa's before realizing what he was doing.

He was looking for Charron. He was just as jittery as the rest of this damnfool town! To hell with what people might think. He was going to get himself a shot!

The day wore on and little serious work was undertaken throughout the sultry morning as folks whittled away their time gossiping, spreading rumours, watching the north trail and speculating endlessly on what could be keeping the governor's man.

Some reasoned he may have been wounded in the gunfight with Jenner and Jackson, might even now be lying dead out along the trail someplace. The telegraph was strangely quiet after its busy, clattering night, and there were more porch loafers and lookouts posted up on the balconies than had been seen since the day

Judge Walker and his retinue arrived from the capital to try Ethan Clay and find him guilty as hell.

Yet ten o'clock came and went, and nobody had sighted a thing. And then, suddenly, he was simply there in full view of all on the shadowed porch of Zampano's Cantina, leaning against an upright with his hat tilted forward and a fuming Dollar cigar clamped between his teeth.

The square was stunned into momentary silence as a hundred citizens stopped and stared.

So far as it was known, nobody in Rio Salto knew the gunman by sight. Yet, somehow, every citizen knew instantly that this had to be him; could only be Ben Charron. For he looked the part from the crown of his rust-brown hat to the heels of his worn, yellow riding boots, and when he lowered a big hand to rest on his shellbelt above a cutaway holster, men tensed uneasily and didn't relax until he finally folded his arms and went on gazing across the hot square like a man with nothing to do and all day to do it.

On the other end of all this attention, Charron quietly enjoyed his cigar and soaked up the atmosphere. He'd deliberately stealthed his way into the town, less to create an impact than out of simple prudence. He'd never been this far south before. Men could be lying for him here. He still didn't know they weren't, although he felt reassured by the atmosphere. There was tension on every side, but no sense of immediate danger. Not yet leastwise.

Then he glanced round at a buzz of voices to see a

tall upright man with a black moustache, and a five-pointed star on his vest, striding towards the cantina with a glitter in his eye that warned him the peace mightn't last.

The tune he blew through his little harmonica was *Por Dios y Libertad* – For God and Liberty. It was well-played, for Ethan Clay had a gift for music in the same way he was a natural horseman and crack shot. He'd picked up the melody during his many forays into Old Mexico, some alone, but mostly with his wild bunch from out along Red Creek. He was lonesome for his pards today, but not overly hopeful of seeing them again here, maybe ever.

The Red Creekers had splintered and taken flight the night stage company boss Ricardo Valdez was shot dead, with Clay subsequently arrested and charged with his murder.

The gang had hideaways, safe houses and holes in the wall sprinkled all over the county. The prisoner alone knew where each man had gone, but there was no way he could contact them yet. All he could do was sweat and pray that the boys would soon all get together again and do what he expected of them, namely come and bust him out of this crackerbox jail before Ramrod Reed and that long-nosed Governor arranged to have him jig and jitter his life away on the end of twelve feet of yellow rope on the Capital's Federation Square.

He abruptly ceased playing. Raised voices sounded

from the front office. Might it be him?

Reed appeared suddenly in the office archway. 'You have a visitor, Clay. Sharpen yourself up.'

'Whatever you say, Mister High Sheriff,' Clay said mockingly, not moving a muscle. Then he blinked as a second figure appeared in the archway, seeming to fill it with his bulk.

'Sonuva!' he muttered beneath his breath, for one glance told him who the second man had to be, who he could only be. Standing there hatless with folded arms, staring at him, he was a jailbird's worst nightmare.

He rose with exaggerated slowness.

' 'Scuse me, Sheriff Reed, sir, but looks like you left your door open and your hoss followed you in.' He waved. 'Shoo! Back outside, Dobbin. Fresh oats!'

'I forgot to mention his sense of humour, Mr Charron,' Reed said coldly. 'It's on a par with his harmonica playing, which is even worse than his singing. I expect you anticipated someone more impressive to have created such a furore?'

Charron came on through the archway to study the prisoner, with a total lack of expression. He saw a man somewhere in his mid-twenties, lean, smart-looking enough, plainly cocky and full of himself, but with a certain weakness around the jawline. Clay winked at him, then blew a perfect smoke ring through the bars which almost made it clear across the annexe before it began to disintegrate.

'Sorry I'm so nervy, but I never did meet a true-blue

honest-to-God gun hero before, Mr Charron, sir.' He chuckled. 'But tell me, ain't there some kind of law against backshooting people, like you did last night? Sheriff, you're the hotshot on the law. Can you shoot men down like dogs and get away with it in this man's county?'

'Hush your mouth!' Reed sounded weary. He drew from his coat pocket the manila envelope containing the official documentation from Capital City authorizing Charron's assignment and demanding he be afforded any assistance and support he may request of any official to expedite the execution of his duty. The papers were endorsed by US Marshal Pearl who had been personally assigned to the territory the previous year by the President of the United States acting upon the advice and consent of the Senate.

'Better keep these,' he grunted to Charron. 'Never know if you might need them again between here and there.'

Charron slipped the envelope into a hip pocket without comment. He and the sheriff had gotten off to a testy start when Reed had revealed he no longer believed Clay to be guilty of the Valdez killing. The lawman had also made it clear that he considered the governor's decision to transport Clay to the Capital to be dealt with to be a crude and naked grab for electoral support. A 'Vote For Me' blood circus was how he described it.

So far he'd allowed the sheriff to do most of the talking. Now it was his turn.

'You still haven't explained how word of my assignment leaked out, Reed. I want to know, seeing as it was

34

top secret between you, me and the governor.'

'Hey, this is great,' Clay chuckled. 'My jailers at one another's throats already. Come on, fight, you bastards, I hate peace.'

'We can discuss this in the office,' Reed said stiffly.

Charron didn't move a muscle. He stood beneath a high barred window with his hat pushed to the back of his head, his wide brown leather gunbelt slanted across his hips, the sleeves of his tan shirt rolled neatly back from powerful forearms.

'My hunch is it had to be you,' he accused bluntly. 'I also reckon I know why. You haven't stopped griping about how you didn't agree with the verdict of the court, or why the district court judge was replaced by another from the bench of the federal court of Southwest Territory. Are you sure you didn't spill your guts in the hope my assignment would fail and you'd get to prove yourself right and the Governor wrong again?'

'I don't have to listen to this,' Reed flared, spinning on his heels. He started for the archway, then halted. 'And for your information, gunman, completion of your assignment, as you call it, is going to be delayed, perhaps considerably.'

Charron's eyes narrowed. 'Meaning?'

'That shootout. Coyoteville's in my area of jurisdiction and I mean to conduct a full investigation to establish that foul play on your behalf was not involved in that one death and one wounding last night.' He strode out, firing back, 'Enjoy your stay in Rio Salto – Mister Special Deputy!'

'Well, well,' Clay snorted. 'If this don't beat the band. Hey, big man, what if old Humph finds out that you gunned Jackson down like a dog, never gave him a chance, or something? We could end up in the clink together. Your pard the Governor might have to send another backshooting son of a bitch like yourself down to escort us both back to the gallows. Wouldn't that be something?'

Charron barely heard. Going out, he paused deliberately to glance round the big airy front office with its walls papered over with wanted dodgers which included, side by side, grainy likenesses of Jenner and Jackson. On another wall, in prominent position, were displayed posters advocating a vote for the democrats would be a vote for progress – surely a breach of regulations in a place where political neutrality was considered obligatory?

The sheriff was at his desk, barking orders at one of the deputies. He expected Charron to speak, but he didn't. Their eyes locked for a long moment. Two strong men engaged in some kind of silent duel. Then it was formidable Humphrey Reed who finally dropped his eyes.

Charron had won, though he was unsure just what that implied.

He went out where the midday sun fell like a hammer across his broad back. The muted strains of a harmonica followed him as he strode across the plaza.

CHAPTER 3

RETURN OF THE HERO

'Is he asleep, Florabelle?' whispered the dark-eyed girl in the transparent pink chiffon.

'How would I know?' grumped Florabelle, eighteen going on forty and badly out of sorts this long, hot afternoon. The number three girl at Mama Tonio's plush establishment on tree-lined Socorro Street, down by Red Creek, folded her plump arms petulantly. 'I ain't been invited in to find out if he's asleep or awake. Nobody has, far as I know.' She scowled as she surveyed the competition in the parlour, five tolerably attractive young women in various stages of undress. 'And nobody else better had, neither. I saw him first. If he's anybody's, he's mine.'

'May I see this one?' the dark-eyed girl said curiously. 'I was not here when he checked in.' She shivered deliciously. 'Is he really so fierce and dangerous?'

'He's big and ugly and he hates women, is what.' Florabelle was far from her best today. Of course, there was nothing wrong with her that an hour or two with a big handsome client wouldn't cure, and she'd thought her prayers were answered around noon when someone fitting that description precisely came rapping on Mama's doorjamb. She'd sniggered knowingly when the fellow told Mama he just wanted a place to rest up away from the people who kept trailing him around, all apparently eager to see what 'the Governor's man' might do next.

Yet sleeping was exactly what he'd been doing all afternoon, and Florabelle was on the verge of denouncing all men and maybe going back to the farm. She went off to discuss this possible career change with Mama, leaving the dark-eyed girl to finger back gently the beaded glass curtain and peer in at this *hombre* who had all of Rio Salto talking.

The almost imperceptible tinkle of curtain beads caused Charron to open one eye and slide his right hand over the handle of the holstered sixshooter hanging from his bed post.

'*Que pasa?*' he demanded. 'What's the matter?'

The girl blinked. With the heavy window drapes drawn tight, his shape was just a dim silhouette on Mama's best bed, the teak one with luxury springs imported from Mexico City for her special clients.

'You are awake, *señor?*'

'No.'

She took a step inside the room. Her dress was totally transparent. He barely noticed. This was one weary rider.

Her whisper turned husky. 'Señor Charron, is it really true that you have come to Mama's to rest?'

'Do you speak Spanish?'

'*Sí.*' Encouraged, she drew a step nearer. 'It is my native tongue.'

'Good. *Voy a mataute!*'

With a small cluck of alarm, the golden-skinned girl fled, the beaded curtains surging violently in her wake. She had just been told very distinctly: 'I am going to kill you.'

He rolled over and closed his eyes again. Two reasons had brought him to the bordello, and neither had anything to do with romance or what passed for it at Mama's. Although he'd secured lodging in clean rooms just off the plaza, he doubted he'd find the immediate peace and quiet there which he knew he could rely upon in a well-run bordello. The chance to catch up on some sleep was his prime objective, his second would be to ask a lot of questions. Experience had taught him that skilled questioning could garner a man more useful information in a whorehouse than almost anyplace else.

He was dreaming of Georgia before the war when yet another intrusion saw him again reaching for the big black Colt. He reholstered with a sigh. No mistaking Mama Tonio's five-by-five silhouette. The good madam resembled a barn door in a floral kimono.

'Is you awake, honeychile?' The voice was as south-ern as sorghum molasses. A waft of powerful scent floated over him as she shook his bare shoulder. 'Mister man, er, what'd yo'all say your name was?'

'*Voy a mataute!*' It had worked once; it was worth a second try.

But this Carolina-born madam of a successful house in the deep south-west, almost on the Mexican border, patriotically and proudly refused to comprehend a single word of Spanish.

She shook him again. Vigorously. 'Ah guess yo' is awake then, honeychile. Better rise up, you got a visi-tor.'

'Forget it.'

'A right purty one at that.'

'Tell her . . . whoever, to go die.'

'Ah cain't go sayin' that to Master McMaster's little chile, now can ah?'

He sat up and swung his bare feet to the floor. 'You talking about Olan McMaster, the cattleman?' Ma nodded and he stood up. McMaster was the biggest man in the county and a close personal friend of the Governor's. Just might be important.

The girls sighed as he padded out through the parlour wearing just long johns and a scowl. On the stoop, where she was being ogled admiringly by a brace of gaudy young *vaqueros* on their way in, he encoun-tered a sexily pretty young woman in rider's denims and open-necked shirt with a basket on one arm, the

40

other extended to him in greeting.

'Oh, Mr Charron,' she smiled, seemingly unfazed by either his attire or the locale. 'Felicity McMaster. I'm so pleased I was able to locate you. I'm not disturbing you, am I?'

'No,' he said deliberately. 'I'm through doing what I came here to do, I guess.'

Either she missed the irony or she really didn't give a damn why he was here. With a brisk shake of his hand, she indicated her basket. 'I have several errands to run this afternoon and I thought perhaps you might like to escort me around while we get acquainted.' Another almost cheeky smile. 'I'm reliably informed that escorting is your profession, or one of them at least. Shall I wait by the gate while you finish dressing?'

He sighed. 'What is it you want, Miss McMaster?'

'Please, Felicity. Well, I just thought you might need a friend in Rio Salto. Badly.' She arched a winged eyebrow. 'A friend who can and will answer many of the questions you must be just dying to ask.'

'What makes you think I'm looking for answers? I'm here to collect a killer, and I know where he is. That's all I need to know.'

'I've just come from the jailhouse where I found Sheriff Reed quite vexed yet impressed that you seem so familiar with so many details about the murder trial and other matters pertaining to both the crime and the unusual circumstances surrounding the court case. He told me you'd obviously studied the transcript of The

People versus Ethan Clay before your arrival. Rather unusual for a gunman just working for the dollar, I feel. Or perhaps I shouldn't use that term? Sheriff Reed claims you were duly sworn in as a special temporary deputy before coming south. By the US Marshal himself, I understand.'

'Let's back up some. You say you visited the jailhouse? How come?'

'Oh, I just stopped by to take Ethan a few tasties, and, you know, a comforting word.'

'Ethan? You know Clay?'

'Of course. He spent several months on the ranch two years ago, breaking horses. Father mistrusts him, but says he's the best horseman he's ever seen.'

'And a killer.'

At that moment Mama Tonio appeared at Charron's side, flashing all her huge white teeth at the girl on the stoop. 'Miz McMaster, maybe it won't do your reputation one bit of good to be seen out here in the eyes of the whole street. You is more than welcome to come inside and—'

'It's OK,' Charron cut in, coming to a decision. 'Just wait here while I put a hat on, Bright Eyes.'

A short time later he found himself making his way for the telegraph office from the bank in company with the ranchero's daughter, a sight to set tongues buzzing all over the placita. The rancher's daughter kept promising to stop for coffee, but then would remember something else she needed to attend to first. This was OK by him. She was sparkling company and drew admiring looks wherever they went. Added to that, she turned out to be as good as her boast insofar as she proved herself a font of information about both Clay and the whole situation down here. Yet he still didn't believe he'd heard the real reason she'd sought him out.

At the office, he fired off a coded wire to Capital City advising the Governor of developments and requesting he do something to get the sheriff out of his hair. Pronto. Feeling fully restored now, he was ready to head north with the prisoner any time, the sooner the better.

He found himself puffing his way through half a cigar on the porch while his companion was busy sending off various wires of her own. He spent the time studying the passing parade, poker-faced and impassive as he traded looks with lithe *vaqueros* sporting black charro with silver conchos, shambling losers from both sides of the border, youthful firebrands and shabby Red Creek supporters who gave him the hard eye, the women who'd given up, and younger ones daring enough to shoot him hot looks which drew no response.

Across on the portico of the hotel, a trio of motionless Mexicans watched him from beneath their secret hatbrims in the sun.

He wasn't immune to any of it, just focused. It was how a man learned to survive in Indian country. He'd survived the desert crossing and an attempt upon his life. If he remained focused, as he'd originally learned

43

how to do through four years of shot and shell, he believed he'd most likely get to survive the return journey with his prisoner intact and pocket his highest ever fee. That was the name of the game.

The fact that the Governor might have hidden motives for wanting to swing Clay personally was no concern of his. He'd always made it a cast-iron rule never to hire out to a man or outfit without first determining they were both honest and lawful. Once that prime essential was established he went ahead and did whatever had to be done to complete the job, regardless of petty details or differences.

When Felicity McMaster finally emerged, all sparkling and full of bounce, she actually linked her arm in his to escort him across the square to an eatery, where he found the coffee powerful but good, and where nobody paid them too much attention.

He wanted to discuss the Clay case some more, and wasn't sure how she steered the conversation round to himself and his journey from the north. Turned out she was familiar with the route he'd taken down, as published in a report in the Rio Salto newspaper. For some reason she seemed curious to know if he intended recrossing the desert again or taking the long way round on his return journey.

He revealed nothing even though his route was mapped out in his head down to the last shade rock and waterhole. It would be the same route he'd followed down. He would recross the desert via Two Holes Trail as far as sun-stricken Holy Ghost Canyon, then strike off due north all the way to the grass plains, via the old Donner Road. Any trail once travelled had to be safer than something new. As for the desert, well, he always felt safer in the wide open country where there were far fewer places for trouble to hide.

He expected her to be cross when he clammed up on her, but once again Felicity McMaster surprised him. 'You're certainly not at all as I expected, Ben Charron,' she told him frankly and without rancour, stirring sorghum into her crockery cup.

'What'd you expect?' She might be pretty and friendly, but he was wary. It was his nature. 'Figured I might shoot someone while we were out promenading?'

'No, not quite that. But I did expect to meet someone far more ruthless and intimidating.'

' Oh, I can be both. Or so I read sometimes.'

'I must confess to reading up on you in the newspaper office files when I first heard you were coming to Rio Salto.' She paused. 'They refer to you as a gunslinger, and worse.'

'Killer?'

'Yes.'

'Nobody's ever hired me to kill a man, never will.'

'But you *have* killed. In your line of work, that is.'

'That's different. I call myself a manhunter. But I'll take on dangerous jobs that nobody else wants.' He shrugged. 'Things happen.'

'Why do you do such work?'

'Someone has to.'

'But why you?'

'I just reckon this country deserves a better deal than it gets, is all.'

'Why, Ben Charron, I swear you sound almost idealistic!'

He took a cigar from his breast pocket. 'You don't think I know what that word means, do you?'

She flushed a little. 'I'm sorry, I . . .'

'Oh, I'm educated, Bright Eyes. I was an officer in the war.' He lit and dragged deep, fixing her with rain-coloured eyes. 'Now, what's this all about? What do you want from me? Well-reared young women don't play up to men of my stamp unless they want something. Tell me what you're after and shock me.'

To his surprise, the daughter of the county's wealthiest citizen proceeded to do just that. She and her father had quarrelled quite seriously over her involvement with a group seeking a retrial for Ethan Clay, she revealed over a second cup of passable joe. She was now determined to journey to Capital City and seek a personal audience with the Governor himself to plead the man's case. But her father, outraged by her defiance, had instructed the stage company not to carry her anyplace for the present, and nobody else would dare assist her and risk McMaster's wrath. She was desperate, and would he help her? Get to the Capital, that was. She felt if Governor Lane had enough confidence in Charron to hire him, then she should be safe enough with him anyplace.

'I'm simply asking if I might travel back north with

you, Ben. I wouldn't be any trouble as I'm a seasoned traveller. And I'd be forever in your debt if you helped me prevent a terrible miscarriage of justice.'

He might have laughed had she been less serious. Instead he simply refused point blank without explanation or apology, tossed money at the waiter and walked out.

He left her in tears at the table. Patrons and staff just shook their heads as if they expected nothing better from his kind.

Ben Charron said, 'Give me another.'

The bartender obliged and Charron turned with the glass in his hand to confront the challenge of the cantina heavyweight who, along with his bunch, had finally taken aboard enough tequila to take him on. Men like the gunman attracted trouble, and in cases like this he liked to meet it head-on. The ox-shouldered bruiser had already called him 'Lane's gun whore' and offered to break his neck, so with the formalities over it was Charron's duty to respond.

Charron threw the liquor in the man's eyes then punched him so hard he took three supporters down with him as he hit the floor with a shattering crash.

The cantina went totally quiet for a breathless handful of seconds, until the sounds of a slow ironic handclap came from over by the piano.

'Bravo!' a voice slurred. 'Hoof, horns and tail to Matador Charron for bringing down the bull. *Olé!*'

A wide gap immediately split the crowd as

47

customers hurried to get clear of the owner of that mocking voice. Charron saw a small table where a drinker sat alone. The man was a compact fellow of around forty with thinning hair and a handlebar moustache which lifted at the corners as he laughed mockingly.

Sudden panic engulfed the smoky room as Charron backed up to the bar and dropped his right hand against the handle of his Colt. His action brought the smaller man to his feet, arms stretched high, the toothy grin still in place.

'Hey, relax, Charron. I'm not bracing you. Hell, man, we both know I've always had your measure, so what'd be the point?' He gestured at the wide-eyed trio on the little podium. 'Let's have some more of that pretty music, amigos. I know, play something appropriate for two old pards getting together after a long spell.'

Only the drummer managed to get a rickety beat going as Charron slowly eased his hand off his gun and watched an old and dangerous associate walk unsteadily toward him, elaborately circling the white-faced patrons attempting to revive the cantina champion with the broken jaw.

To mark their 'fortuitous reunion', as he termed it, Doc Christian drank down three whiskies over the next half-hour, during which time the town medic showed up to work on the blacksmith for some time before they toted him out lying on a door, still unconscious and looking like death, his former friends now nowhere to be seen.

Content to allow Christian to do most of the talking, Charron worked his way through a Dollar cigar and toyed with his lucky charm, the tiny metal figurine of a woman in a long robe, attached to his right wrist by a fine silver chain.

'*Salud,*' the other grunted every so often, and drank his whiskey down.

They dated back to Abilene in the last year of the great cattle drives which wound up from Texas via the Chisholm Trail to the railhead. Doc had really been something then: gambler, raconteur, reporter for a big eastern paper, a dab hand with women and lethal talent with a sixshooter.

Through one long Kansas summer they'd both courted the same woman, and watching this triangular affair played out against the backdrop of the wildest town in the West, self-styled experts on romance and gunplay had speculated endlessly on which man would come out of it alive if their rivalry ever exploded into a .45 showdown.

But Charron the manhunter, who loathed the gunslinger tag men had given him, never drew on any man unless his life was threatened. Nor would he risk losing Terasina, which he knew would be the outcome were he ever to get to duel the Doc over her.

So he continued on as a highly paid backup to the City Marshal in the town's season-long war with a thousand trail-crazed Texans, maintained an edgy friendship with Christian and for a time seriously entertained thoughts of marrying the first woman he'd ever loved.

49

Terasina Moreno.

Even after all this time, the thought of her brought a gentle ache, for it had been an unforgettable summer with he and her secret lovers, and a proud but hopeful Doc tagging along for the ride.

All three rented quarters at the Drover's Cottage, biggest hotel on the plains with a hundred large airy rooms, barn and corral space for fifty carriages and a hundred horses. Virtually every big cattleman in the West checked in at the Cottage one time or another.

Content to allow the marshal to handle most of the gun work involved in suppressing the always simmering violence in the town, Charron – maybe softened by romance for the first time in his life – got through that turbulent season barely firing a shot in anger.

Upon windswept streets and beneath trembling saloon lamps, he perfected the art of buffaloing liquor-crazed cowpokes with a gunbutt, or simply manhandling them out of action just as they were working up to try something of the foolish or fatal kind.

At the height of the danger season, Doc Christian signed on to back his play and they formed a formidable team, and mostly when there was shooting to be done, Doc handled it. The gun business excited this complex little man in a way it never had Charron.

Christian came whisper close to calling Charron out the day Terasina finally made it clear that it was Ben she loved, not him. Paradoxically, this announcement came shortly after the lovers' final rift, when the Spanish beauty finally realized that Ben would never hang up the guns. Could not, would not. And had made it clear that he would never condemn any woman to a life tied to a man who risked his life almost daily.

He'd not seen Christian since that day, and how things had changed. Doc was now an unashamed drunk. He didn't work any more, just played cards and drank his whiskey straight. There had always been a cynical world-weary edge to his character, and this was now accentuated. He was a bitter man and more dangerous than ever, Charron sensed. He'd been resident here for three months, was plainly waiting for Charron to ask him why, seeing as how Rio Salto was certainly no tourist stopover.

But Charron was saying very little about anything. So finally Doc ordered a double and said softly, 'Saw her a couple of weeks back, Ben.'

Charron stiffened. 'Who?'

'You know who.'

'Where? How. . . ?'

'She lives to the south. Runs an eatery. Not married. Doesn't that beat all, a gorgeous hunk of hot-bodied woman like that?'

Charron made no reply. Terasina was an open wound. It was she who'd given him the figurine of the Virgin which hung from his wrist. On the night after they'd parted for the last time, he'd sat alone on a wrought iron balcony in Cairo overlooking the Mississippi. Whenever the breeze off the river gusted, another streetlight seemed to blow out. He sat there until the whole city lay in darkness, listening to the slow painful thudding of his heart and staring emptily into the bleak years ahead.

She had tried to understand why he could never quit. She was the only living person in whom he'd confided the strange motivation for the life he'd chosen for himself after the war. Yet she still did not fully comprehend it, and he did not blame her. Christian, clever enough to figure what drove him to a life behind the gun, mockingly called him a 'crusader'. Charron rejected the term, yet liked it better than 'killer'.

'Cheer up, man,' Christian said with forced heartiness. 'She knows you're here.'

Charron blinked slowly. 'What?'

'When word that you were coming down to visit with us poor folks was shouted from every rooftop, she wired me to ask if it was true.' He spread his hands. 'She'd know you're here by now. Everybody else does. She'll come, I know it. Maybe I always understood her better than you.'

'Maybe you did at that.'

Something about Charron's unshakeable composure brought a hot flush to Christian's ruined face.

'You still think you're God Almighty, don't you?' he accused bitterly. 'Well, it just could be your days are numbered – crusader! This whole grandstand caper of coming down here alone after a mean bastard like Clay, who every ragged-ass loser looks up to just because he can bust broncs and get any female he wants, near got you killed at Coyoteville up north and surely will finish you if you don't get wise and wire home for some gun backing. But you're too big for that, aren't you? Well, let them get you. Who gives a rat's ass?'

'Would that make you feel better if they did? Get me, that is?'

'Yesss!'

The smaller man's enmity had finally cracked the façade of his indifference.

'All right, Christian, at least I know where you stand. Now I'll tell you where I stand. I'll do what I came to do and if any man tries to stop me, I'll kill him. That includes you.'

'Kill me? You forget I'm as good as you!'

'You mean as bad, don't you?'

'Killin's bad? You saying that? Oh sure, you just hate the kill, I don't think.'

A pause, then, 'She was always too good for you!' Christian almost yelled, and a silent, staring crowd had no notion who or what they were quarrelling about.

'Still stuck on her yourself, eh, Doc?'

'Go to hell.'

'Best you can do? You've slipped a long way. The way you're drinking, you could be dead in a year.'

'So? You could be dead by midnight.'

Suddenly Charron wanted another shot of that smooth brandy. But rules were rules. He not only lived by them, he'd made them his credo.

He threw money upon the bartop. 'Have one on me, Doc. For old time's sake.'

53

Christian swiped the coins to the floor. 'I'll never need a drink that bad.'

'Suit yourself.'

He turned to go. But the other's words halted him.

'Hey, how come Jenner and Jackson anyway?'

'What?'

'Not that I give a cuss, but I've got to say I was plenty surprised when I heard how it was those hotshots jumped you. It takes big money to retain the likes of them. Serious money. Any notion who could be bankrolling your funeral?'

'Would I tell you if I did?'

'Same old Charron.' Doc's eyes appeared watery. No venom in that ruined face now. 'Will I give her your love if I see her?'

But Charron was gone, the thud of his boot-heels first loud then fading to silence on the warped porch-boards beyond the windows.

'To the return of the hero!' Doc Christian yelled mockingly. And held his empty glass high.

CHAPTER 4

THE GOVERNOR'S MAN

The first roosters were crowing as Charron quit his rooming-house with his warbag slung over his shoulder, moving quietly through the half dark to the lamplit stables. The horse whickered a greeting from the stables and he was soon leading the animal across the shadowed plaza as the last stars faded above the church.

The jailhouse was ablaze with light as was the case every morning at this time, likewise the stage station. His thoughts focused on his pending confrontation with the sheriff and he was only dimly aware that the overnight stage had rolled into the depot yard with hands bustling about the landing and hostlers changing the team. He paused to observe idly the figures moving to and fro, the passengers and crew stretching their legs after the forty mile run up from the south. One passenger, a well-dressed woman, was descending on to the plankwalk followed by a stagehand toting her valise.

Charron took three more steps then stopped on a dime. Staring across at that slim figure again, he felt a jolt of recognition. Tall and stately in quaker cloth grey and a Spanish *rebozo* drawn over raven hair, there was something regal about this woman's bearing that was surely unique.

He felt his breath catch in his throat.

Terasina!

Instantly the years since Abilene slipped by as though they'd never happened. It was if he was rooted to the spot as he watched the woman suddenly stop as though sensing a presence, then turn sharply to see him standing tall and dark against the light mouse-grey of the grulla.

'Ben!'

The sleepy-eyed padre didn't seem to mind when the couple entered his dimly lit church and occupied a pew towards the rear. The woman's face glowed with pleasure at first, but the gunman was grave and stern.

'I heard you were here. Ben, I . . . I just had to come and see you. You look wonderful, but then you always did.' She took his hands in hers in a gesture that went

56

back to that Abilene summer when he'd dared dream of a future away from the streets and the stink of gunsmoke. Yet before that violent season was over, he'd come to realize that he was committed to the life, and it was not one any man would want to share with a woman he loved.

'Ben, you're not saying anything. Are . . . are you sorry I came?'

'I'm sorry, Terasina. Nothing's changed.'

Later, he clearly remembered saying those words, but little of what was said afterwards. She took it well, of course. She was at once the strongest and gentlest woman he'd ever known. And it was like the pain of Abilene all over again.

Afterwards, their brief time together from that moment onwards in the stone church on the Plaza of Heroes would come back to him as a blurred recollection of stilted words and awkward silences, fragments of disjointed time slipping by painfully, the one thing sharply recalled with knife-edged clarity later was the agony of knowing it was finally and irrevocably over.

He could feel her withdrawing from him even though she still sat close on the worn polished pew, which was beneath a plaster saint clutching a rosary, gazed down upon them with shadowed eyes from a wall niche.

'Well, my hopes were not high, *caballero*,' she admitted with dignity and candour. 'And it is wonderful to see you again, even if . . .'

Her voice trailed away. Always perceptive and intuitive

where he was concerned, she'd realized virtually instantly that the man she loved appeared if anything even more driven and committed to his private 'cause' than had been the case in Abilene.

It was little comfort to Terasina Moreno to know that she alone of all the people who passed through his life knew what drove him to live as he did.

There were no tears, no recriminations. They were strong people, both adept at controlling their emotions. Abilene had proven a fiery crucible of experience which had tempered them both, and there was almost an old-fashioned formality in the way in which he escorted her back across the morning square to the depot landing and the porter waiting patiently with her luggage. Then formally shaking her hand . . . goodbye . . .

'I'm sorry I must go, Terasina. It's something that can't wait.'

'It always was. But I understand, Ben. *Por favor*, take special care. I know the danger of your assignment here. Do promise you will at least take care.'

'I'll be fine,' he replied, holding up the tiny figurine. 'Your Lady looks out for me. *Adios*.'

'*Vaya con Dios*.'

She stood on tiptoes and kissed him fully on the mouth before turning swiftly away.

He had no recollection of leading the horse to the far side of the square and tying it up next door to the jailhouse. But by the time he'd finished haggling over the purchase of a bay horse and saddle with the sleepy liveryman, and led the saddled animal out into the daylight, he was whole again, solid, the old aching hurt back where it belonged. Locked away.

Tying the mount up alongside the grulla at the jailhouse hitchrail, he mounted the porch steps. He nodded to the deputy posted by the front door and entered the front office.

'I've come to take delivery of my prisoner,' he stated quietly as Humphrey Reed glanced up from his desk. 'That means right now.'

The sheriff came slowly to his feet, his expression confounded. 'How in hell did you know?' he asked to Charron's puzzlement. The lawman was holding a yellow telegraph slip between thumb and forefinger. 'This only arrived minutes ago.'

Charron frowned. 'What is it?'

Reed proffered the slip. 'Why, Marshal Pearl's official order instructing me to turn Clay over to your custody immediately, of course. See for yourself.'

He scanned the message at a glance. He might have grinned at the irony of it at another time. Overnight, he'd decided that he would take custody of the prisoner, at gunpoint if need be, and had arrived at the jail prepared to do just that. But plainly Capital City had also grown as impatient with the sheriff's delaying tactics as he had, and so he wouldn't need to consider the .45 option after all.

'Bring him out,' he ordered the senior deputy. He folded the paper and slung it back to the sheriff. Humphrey Reed looked disconsolate, although he remained argumentative.

'I'm not letting this matter rest here, deputy, if that's what you're supposed to be called.' He sniffed, a vain, overbearing man accustomed to getting his own way. But not today. 'You can tell that to the marshal, the Governor and the Federal judge from me. They all know full well there was insufficient evidence to convict this man and—'

'You've played that tune to death, mister,' Charron chipped in. 'And it doesn't take too many smarts to figure what's behind your attitude.'

'Meaning?'

'Politics, mister – politics and ambition. You reckon I don't know you haven't been pressing for a town patent for Rio Salto ever since you got elected? Or that you expect to be promoted chief executive when Rio Salto does eventually become the county seat? Or that everybody and his dog doesn't know you're a rabid Democrat and want to see a Republican governor ousted? That's why you first arrested Clay for murder, then changed your tune when Capital City showed interest in the case. You didn't want to give Governor Lane the boost he's sure to get by making an example of Clay; you wanted to undermine the whole Clay case so as to make Lane look bad and maybe cost him the election.'

The sheriff of Rio Salto turned pale.

'You really believe that, don't you?'

'What's it matter what I believe? I know your breed, mister. Little men wanting to be big. I meet them everyplace. And you don't give a rap if you have to subvert the law you're sworn to serve to get what you want. If I was Lane I'd fire you and haul you to the Capital to face an investigation into your handling of the entire case.'

'You're so wrong, gunslinger—'

'Forget that tag, pilgrim, it doesn't fit. What I am is somebody who more often than not gets assigned jobs to patch up the mess self-seekers like you stir up, instead of concentrating on making this country as good as it deserves to be.'

'All right, all right,' Reed said placatingly, intimidated despite himself. 'But before you go you should be reminded of exactly what happened here. Señor Ricardo Valdez was murdered by the Red Creek bunch the night he caught them robbing his hacienda outside of town. We were alerted and got there in time for a shootout. We caught Clay attempting to run off some prime stock and later charged him with the murder. It was a week before one of the hands recovered sufficiently from being shot up to inform us that he was close by the hacienda when Valdez was gunned down by another of the raiders, name of Krile. The hand swore it was a good five minutes before Clay came galloping back to the headquarters from the horse-yards a mile away.'

He paused for effect.

'He couldn't have killed anybody,' he went on. 'Now can you understand why I wanted the charges dropped? And I know you're aware the circuit judge was ready to support my belief in Clay's innocence

61

until the Governor suddenly replaced him with his Federal Judge Omar Burlinson off the bench of the Capital's District 31. Clay is not guilty, dammit! It's got nothing to do with politics!'

'Bravo, Sheriff, you tell him straight!' interrupted the mocking voice of Ethan Clay.

The deputy had emerged from the cell annexe with the manacled prisoner at his side. Clay clapped his hands and grinned from ear to ear. Charron motioned both men outside before turning back to a pale-faced Reed.

'I'll take the advice of a Federal court judge over a town sheriff any day of the week, mister. But don't be fretting about Clay, start worrying about yourself. You're still my prime suspect for leaking word on my assignment all over Rosanna County. If that can be proved, the next time we meet you could be behind bars.'

The sheriff was ashen. 'Why, you cheap—'

'Killer?' Charron spun on his heels. 'There's worse tags than that. Try corrupt lawman.'

He went out to find the square suddenly crowded. Bad news travels fast and it seemed half of Rio Salto was now on hand to witness Clay's departure. Chains and cuffs didn't prevent the prisoner blowing a jaunty tune through his harmonica, and a scatter of onlookers managed a feeble cheer for this show of bravado. Although almost everyone Charron had encountered in Rio Salto was out to see them leave, there was no sign of either Terasina Moreno or Felicity McMaster as the two riders made their slow way across the square unimpeded.

Something he did see, however, was the small knot of punters gathered before the saloon on the South Street corner. The host of the Lazy Rider was running a book on the Clay affair, and was forced to erase hastily his quoted odds and chalk in revised figures on his porch blackboard as the two horsemen quit the square without incident and receded along the desert trail.

Clay was now at short odds to hang whereas just yesterday he'd been even money.

High summer in the arid lands and desperadoes were riding.

From the South came the tow-headed Dutchman with the limp, a shirt stuffed with wanted dodgers and five crude notches hacked into the scarred walnut stock of his sawn-off shotgun.

From the West came the youthful half-breed outlaw who'd grown to manhood wild and untamed with Ethan Clay; the man who'd vowed either to save his pard from the gallows or to give up the owlhoot and take up minding the door at Mama Tonio's in Rio Salto as penance should he fail.

The two younger men swinging down the northeast trail were the dark-eyed Garcia twins, longtime thorns in the side of the law in Rosanna County even prior to the Valdez killing which had resulted in the Red Creek gang scattering to the four winds.

63

Last but not least, the tall, hard-riding man with maverick stamped all over him was forking an eighteen-hand Sioux gelding through the Paiute Hills along Cattle Fork Road. Oldest of the bunch and wanted for murder in Mexico, this lone rider regarded himself as the real leader of the bunch and a cut above hellers like the breed, or flashy grandstanders like Clay.

But, unlike the Dutchman, Slinger Dunne and the Garcias, who had all been holed up quietly in remote little hideouts during their temporary exile, tough Krile was coming home with big news. For in a remote Mexican hill town, he'd found himself in the unexpected company of a brand new friend whose bloody reputation made the Red Creek gang look like a bunch of schoolkids by comparison. Too bad, mused Reuben Krile, that when he'd received his anticipated coded telegram emanating from Rio Salto on the same day as his henchmen got theirs, resulting in all five immediately taking to the trails, his new notorious buddy was still recovering from an almost fatal shooting, otherwise he'd have readily joined the five.

The Red Creek gang would rendezvous somewhere out in the desert.

Dalton sat down with a grunt, a big sweating man with a heavy gold watchchain slung across a too-tight waistcoat. He was an ex-cattleman with a broken nose whose official designation here in Capital City was deputy governor, and adviser on beef, trade and transport. He was discontented, overbearing, ambitious and knew most of the tricks associated with getting people elected, or, as should be the case very shortly, trying to get Governor Matherson Lane re-elected for a second term.

The varnished door across the big room led directly to the Governor's office, where Dalton fiercely believed he belonged; Governor Dalton, with Matherson Lane relegated to a corner desk out here with the would-bes.

But the territorial Governor had no intention of trading places with an ambitious deputy, or indeed any of the dozen candidates running against him in the pending election. He'd fought ruthlessly to get where he was and was determined to retain power, even if at this moment, towards the end of yet another taxing day of work and heat, he was far more preoccupied with simply finishing up and getting back to the relative coolness of his quarters below than with the large matter of political survival.

Lane was a tired man by sundown. Setting down his pen, he pressed forefinger and thumb to the corners of his eyes and sat motionless, willing the stress away. He was a patrician fifty-year-old with steel-grey hair and a military bearing that was a legacy of West Point. A career soldier until the seventies, the former general had swept into power in a landslide election four years earlier, but those days of heady popularity were long gone.

During his term, the Territory had acquired its sobriquet as 'Outlaw Territory'. He was now campaigning on a law and order platform despite the fact – or perhaps because of it – that outlawry was on the increase throughout the south-west. Enemies and rivals contended that it was the power he loved, not the people. He didn't give much of a damn what they believed. He was the Governor of the Territory, and they weren't.

But even a lax and out-of-touch leader had to be prepared to give of his best with election day just round the corner. There were petitioners and voters to see, meetings to sit through, strategies to formulate, an endless flood of detail and minutiae requiring his personal attention.

He sighed and rang his little brass desk bell. He was standing by the windows staring out at the territorial flag hanging limp and motionless in the dead air of the courtyard when Dalton entered.

'You rang, Governor?'

He didn't turn. 'What news from Rosanna County?'

Dalton knew exactly what he meant.

'Charron is on his way at last, sir.'

'With our man, of course?'

'Sure.'

Some of the tension eased from Lane's shoulders. He swung round and fixed his subordinate with the eye of a soldier, clear and far-seeing.

'Then we should expect to see him . . . when? Three days? Four, perhaps?'

'Could be three, all going well.'

'That being the case, I presume you are ready to

concede that my decision to have Marshal Pearl keep this whole extradition operation low-key and contained was the correct one?'

Dalton rested a beefy ham on a corner of the huge cherrywood desk. The two argued often; they'd argued heatedly over the Governor's decision to commission Charron for the Rio Salto assignment.

'Maybe.'

Dalton was cautious tonight. Lane was yet to nominate his deputy for the next administration. Dalton wanted the job so bad he could taste it. To get it he believed he must play the diplomat over the weeks ahead. He added mildly, 'I guess we can count ourselves lucky Charron survived, huh? Assassins don't come any deadlier than Harlan Jenner and Jackson. Or expensive, so I'm told. Marshal Pearl would give his eye teeth to hang 'em both, the blood they've got on their hands.'

'At least one's dead and the other was badly wounded, according to reports,' Lane replied, crossing the carpet to the north windows overlooking Federation Square. 'But I agree that someone paid out a great deal of money to prevent Charron completing his assignment. Who would your chief suspect be?'

Dalton shrugged.

'Pick any name of a dozen. Could have been our Democrat rivals. Or it might've been one of those crackpot outfits down south eager to free Clay so's to make us look bad. Could be anyone with big dollars. Anyway, as you say, Charron put Jackson in the ground and there hasn't been a word on Jenner since Coyotero, so he could be dead, too. Good riddance, I say.'

There was a hint of a cooling breeze coming across the great square, and suddenly the Governor felt a revival of his energies.

'I'm going to take a turn of the town, Strat. Want to join me?'

Dusk was falling as the two tall men made their way across the square past the flower sellers' barrows, the stalls and markets where you could buy anything from a hat pin to a hayrack. The air was thick with the smells of frijoles frying, horses, humanity and poverty. Moving through the racket of dispute, discussion and sharp dealing, they paused at the foot of an unpainted plank edifice rising gauntly some fifteen feet above its broad wooden base with wide steps leading up to the sinister outline of a gallows rearing tall against the twilight sky.

People kept tacking up 'Free Ethan Clay' posters around the gibbet, and the deputies, troopers and regulators kept removing them. Largely known only as a renowned horseman and troublemaker this far north until a month ago, the publicity Clay had attracted had somehow seen the man elevated to the unlikely status of a folk hero representing almost everybody with a gripe against the government.

Lane didn't slacken pace until he attained his objective. The open grass plain surrounding the capital reached away across all the flat miles out to the frowning, dramatic bulk of the Dinosaur Mountains whose jagged peaks still burned crimson from the setting sun against the backdrop of a darkening sky.

Out here, briefly but invigoratingly, the Governor felt free of all the burdens of his office and was always better able to envision his future, climbing higher, always higher, with the assistance of carefully hand-picked professionals such as Dalton, Marshal Pearl and, yes, even a different kind of pro like Ben Charron who, right at that moment if his calculations were accurate, should be well on his way north with his prisoner.

He would win his second term, he told himself in those rare moments of complete relaxation. He was prepared to do anything to win his second term, even hang a nobody who might well be innocent for all anybody knew.

His game plan was to win big, boost his national standing, move on to a seat in Congress, and who could say how far he might climb from there?

He turned to look back at the city, the lights on now, evening noises replacing the clamour of commerce. Squinting, he realized he could just discern the light-lined upper section of the upright and the crossbeam of the gallows against a velvet sky.

Too bad about Clay, he mused, but without any real sympathy. But it was a fact both of life and of power politics that whenever the really big games were played out by the major players, somebody had to lose. More often than not it was the innocent.

CHAPTER 5

CANYON OF THE HOLY GHOST

The horses blew softly through their noses and jingled their harnesses as they rubbed their heads against their legs to mop up the running sweat.

'Just look at those pokes,' Clay snorted derisively. 'Not an hour since we quit Coyoteville and they're boogered already.' He gestured. 'So am I, for that matter—'

'Mount up.'

'But—'

'I won't say it twice.'

With an exaggerated groan, Ethan Clay got up. Charron followed suit, eyes on the ground, sniffing the hot wind, occasionally lifting his big head to squint north in the direction they were headed. Times like this he was more Apache scout than white man; sighting, sifting his sensations, suspecting where there was no apparent need for suspicion.

Clay rode ahead with shoulders slumped, yet paradoxically he was smirking in the deep black shadow of his hat, his eyes quick and cunning as they ranged expectantly ahead over a hostile landscape.

Another hour's travel and they were in the real desert wilderness of sandhill, mesquite and wind-blown brush with an occasional gaunt stone spire rising starkly into the bleached sky and casting its shadow over arid mesa and decade-dry creekbed. Keeping to the faint trace of the almost invisible Two Holes Trail, they clop-hoofed through ankle-deep dust that soaked up all sound with only the occasional snort of a horse or the tinkle of a harness to disturb the silence.

Until Charron's grulla tossed its head and pricked its ears sharply just as they started up a gaunt and rocky saddle in the trail where the skeleton of a gila monster was baking on a basalt rock.

Immediately he drew level with his prisoner and ordered him to rein in. He stepped down and looped the lines over his horse's head before drawing his rifle from its scabbard, the soft kid leather folding when the stiffness was gone.

'Step down and walk across the trail and stay put while I reconnoitre,' he said tersely. 'You don't move and you don't make a sound. *Compre*?'

'Whatever you say, big man. You're the boss, like you keep remindin' me.'

If Ethan Clay Should Hang

Boot-heels sucking in alkali, Charron made his wary way to the crest and immediately sighted the figure of a young woman standing in the sparse shade of a petrified tree a hundred yards below in a trailside gully-wash, her leather-topped buggy with its empty shafts resting on the burning earth close by.

His jaw dropped. 'What in the blue hell . . ?'

Felicity McMaster seemed to hear. Her head turned and her heat-reddened face lit up like a Christmas tree when she sighted him framed against the bleached sky.

'Ben, oh Ben!' she cried. 'Is it really you?'

Without waiting for a response she came running towards him. She was dressed for the outdoors now, snug-fitting jeans and calico blouse unbuttoned at the throat. Resting the butt of the Winchester on his boot, Charron fingered his hat off his forehead to release the pent-up sweat there. At a sound from behind he glanced over his shoulder to see Clay concentrating on the match flame cupped in his hands as he lifted it to his freshly rolled cigarette.

'Ben, Ben,' the girl gasped as she reached him. 'Oh my stars, am I glad to see you! I knew I was being foolish. . . crazy perhaps. . . but you see I just had to reach the Capital quickly, and I knew you'd come this way safely, but I forgot how dangerous it was and—'

'All right, calm down and start from the beginning,' he cut in, already starting back down the slope. He was angry but tried not to let it show, his thoughts already leaping ahead, trying to slot this unexpected develop-

72

ment into the timeframe of the journey stretching before them.

Felicity McMaster was apologetic, shamefaced. She sipped water thirstily from Charron's canteen when they reached the horses. She occasionally fielded a question from a wryly amused Clay while relating her story.

She made it brief and simple. She'd decided to make the desert crossing, but her horse had been scared off by a snake and left her stranded.

Her apologetic smile seemed ineffectual against the wall of Charron's silence. She looked uncertain. 'I do hope I haven't ruined your plans. What . . . what will you do with me?'

'Take you back to Coyoteville, of course.' It was a threat but an empty one, he knew. He couldn't really afford an hour's delay, much less a couple of days. She'd have to go with them.

The girl attempted to hug him when he announced his decision, but backed off when she caught his expression. He was mad clear through, suspicious also. Yet by the time he'd seen to the mounts, harnessed the buggy to his reluctant grulla and seen the prisoner mounted up again, he was more accepting of the situation. After all, on the credit side, she was pretty, spirited, and brave as a Kiowa horse-soldier as demonstrated by her coming out here alone.

Yet not for a moment was he forgetting what else she was, namely a fierce believer in his prisoner's innocence.

He drew her aside before they climbed into the rig.

'I want you to get something straight from the start, Bright Eyes. I don't trust you, knowing how you feel about Clay. So, if it so much as enters your head to try and help him, you could wind up dead. I've never shot a woman, but by the same token I've never not delivered a party I'm responsible for. You've been warned fair.'

'Oh, Ben Charron, I just love the way you say that.'

'What? That I'll kill you if I have to?'

'No, the way you call me Bright Eyes.'

'Get moving, Clay.'

As the cavalcade set off toward a far-reaching plain studded with endless clusters of barren rockpiles, Charron caught Clay in an unguarded moment studying him sideways from beneath his tilted hat brim. The man's eyes were shaded, yet some light in their depths made them vivid; light but dangerous, wild with desperation.

He nodded to himself as they climbed round a rise. That captured glance served as a timely warning against complacency. He had Ethan Clay tagged as personable but lightweight, but just maybe he could be more.

Night came down fast and hard, but they kept on, as little pebbles rattled beneath iron-shod hoofs and rubber-tyred wheels.

'Can you see where we're going?' Felicity said in his ear, just the slightest echo of little-girl unease in her tone now.

'Sure.'

'I suspect you always see.'

'It's a gift.'

She didn't seem to catch the irony in his voice. They travelled steadily onwards with a towering overhang of raven-haunted rocks at their backs.

'You have got to be joshin', Charron. No fire out here in the middle of the freakin' desert? Fel, talk to your boyfriend, will you? Maybe it's so long since he felt anythin' at all that now he can't even feel it when it's down around zero and gettin' colder by the minute.'

Standing wrapped in a blanket from the buggy, Felicity didn't seem to hear the prisoner's lament. She too was cold as the first glimmer of frozen moonlight touched the fantastic rock shapes surrounding Holy Ghost Canyon. They all were. But for the moment she was too absorbed, even intimidated, by the prehistoric landscape surrounding them.

'Is this where you camped on your way south, Ben?' she wanted to know, clenching her teeth to prevent their chattering.

'Yeah.'

'But why?' She shuddered. 'This place would scare a saint.'

'Water's the reason.' He was attending the horses farther along the broad shelf of rock where he'd set up camp. 'It's a long rough climb down to the spring. We'll fill up everything at daylight and should make it to the grasslands by dark down. Better get some rest.'

'I simply can't believe anybody could rest in this place, especially by night. Have you ever been out here before, Ethan?'

'I've been everywhere God's got land, momma.'

'Seriously.'

'Everywhere God's got land, and all I've ever met was folks with hard ways to go.'

Clay's 'preacher man' voice came out from a deep pocket of shadow beneath an overhang where Charron had shackled him after attending to his needs. He sounded cocky for some reason Charron couldn't figure.

The campsite straddled a ledge roughly halfway down to the canyon wall where the distant tinkle of running water could be faintly heard below. He'd have taken them down all the way had not darkness overtaken them; the trail was too steep to travel by moonlight.

Holy Ghost Canyon gouged its erratic course across a sun-blasted plain roughly at the centre of the desert. Few travellers ever came this way, for obvious reasons. By day it might well have been the hottest place in fifty miles, by night surely the coldest.

Charron liked the place. It was a place of extremes and he'd been called extreme many a time. He shook the thought away as his horse whickered behind him.

'What is it, boy?'

'Now he's talking to his horse.' Clay spoke normally now, a hunched shape against light-coloured rock. 'We freeze our asses off, we can't light a fire because he's

76

scared the Holy Ghost might get riled, we got a woman half-dead from the cold and—'

'I'm all right,' Felicity broke in. 'Honestly, don't worry about me.' A pause, then, 'But what a mug of coffee wouldn't taste like . . .'

Her voice broke off. She was shivering too hard to talk. With a frown, Charron crossed to her and rested the back of his hand against her cheek. She was freezing. He looked behind him where the large cave was just an indistinct black mass. Maybe he was being too cautious.

Felicity jumped up and down with excitement and Clay applauded by clanking his manacles together when he announced they could have a fire and coffee. Not all night, he warned, but maybe for an hour or two.

Ignoring their enthusiasm, he went scouting. Fuel was scarce, yet soon he had a good fire going with coffee on the boil. He left the girl in charge of fixing the beverages while he checked out the animals one last time and reassured himself everything was quiet, just as it should be.

When he returned to the fire he found Clay halfway through his coffee, but Felicity had saved hers to share with him. They sat on rocks opposite the small blaze and he drank deep.

'If it tastes a little different, I added some sorghum from my bag in the buggy,' the girl smiled.

'Yeah, it's different,' he said, taking another swig. 'But drinkable.'

He frowned.

'I guess . . .' he added, staring into his mug.

'Something's not right . . .' he began to say and made to rise, but for some reason he almost lost his balance. He steadied himself and stared down at the girl, still seated upon her rock. She returned his look with a smile. But the smile was too fixed, her stare too intent.

'What is it, Ben?'

Her words resonated hollowly from the high walls. He stared down at the coffee still in his hand and felt something stir in his belly, like he was going to be sick.

'Coffee!' he said, his voice sounding thick even to his own ears. He blinked at the girl again and she wasn't smiling now. Now his head began to spin and there was a spreading numbness in his feet and hands. The mug slipped from his hands and bounced on the rock. He began reeling backwards, fumbling awkwardly for his gun. 'You little bitch!' he slurred, knowing now, understanding hitting him with the force of a piledriver.

He'd been doped. She'd spiked the coffee!

His heel caught in a crack in the rock and he fell heavily, crashing down hard on one shoulder. He heard strange voices as he rolled, but they were indistinct, vibrating. He felt cold stone against his cheek. With a mighty act of will he surged upwards with what remained of his strength to find himself swaying drunkenly with the cliffs and that great mellow moon and stars all whirling and blurring in his vision while his mind hammered out a single message in the echoing cavern of his skull: DANGER!

He couldn't see straight, barely knew who he was, or

where. But now there were other sounds, shouting, different voices, the blurred outlines of rushing figures, a woman's voice screaming, 'No, put away your guns! You promised!'

He ran.

His head was roaring and the sickness clawed at his guts. He was dimly conscious of the risk in running blindly along the high ledge, but the sense of a greater danger was stronger. He was drunk, giddy, off-balance and barely able to distinguish light from dark. But the voices and the hammering thud of his heartbeat combined to keep the warning bell clamouring until everything else was overtaken by a thunderous clap of noise that sounded to his ears like dynamite going off underwater.

He felt a sharp kiss of pain along his shoulder cap as he swerved to avoid a pillar of rock, and knew he'd been shot. He propped and blasted three deafening shots at a rushing figure with light-coloured hair. The figure howled and plunged over the edge. He heard a woman's high-pitched scream as he slewed about to run again. Then the earth was giving way beneath his feet and he was tumbling end over end as he rode downwards on a river of cascading rock and earth.

Several times he passed out during that brutal slide, but each time he partially recovered consciousness he was grateful to realize he was still rolling down an earthslide and not free falling to the canyon floor.

Then his head slammed something unyielding which brought him to a jarring halt with every last ounce of air belted from his body. He groaned once and tried to move before the world turned black.

Charron lay half-buried in a pile of dirt and rubble, but didn't know it. Like a diver coming up from the depths he was rising through ever-lightening levels of consciousness towards a slowly strengthening light until his momentum finally slowed then ceased. In some drug-dimmed recess of his brain he thought he had regained consciousness. But it was only an illusion. His recovery had been stalled, yet there was a momentary recognition of danger and pain before his eyelids fluttered and he found himself in a cornfield beneath the gentlest morning sun the world had ever seen.

It was no ordinary cornfield. Instead of nodding yellow husks, only the jagged bayonets of broken stalks fanged this innocent sky. No birdsongs, just a silence as deep as the river of time.

Then, as he raised his head, the big young man wearing the tattered, blood-caked grey of a Confederate guerrilla officer knew with certainty that he was in Tennessee and it was 16 December 1864, a short and fateful time after General Hood's grey army had stood menacingly before Nashville, and now confronted Thomas's blue legions at a place named Overton Hill.

Initially unstoppable as they surged up the hill, before the Federals could reach the heavily defended crest, they were received by a tremendous fire of Rebel grapes, canisters and musketry which drove them back with heavy losses.

Before that day, many pitched battles both large and small were fought, and Ben Charron was amongst the warriors . . .

The young soldier rose from the soft earth as if in a dream to see the sleeper lying before him. The soldier wore Union blue and his unlined face was turned child-like towards the rising sun.

Charron blinked and there was another sleeper close by. Another boy – or he seemed like a boy to the eyes of a war-scarred veteran of the Georgian Guerrillas. This sleeper wore Confederate grey and a trickle of red traced down his youthful jawline that had never felt the touch of a razor.

Then another face, another and another.

So silent it was like standing in the hush of a cathedral. No rustle of corn, no sound of his own movements as he rose to full height to realize that this entire cornfield enclosed by a shattered grey fence was filled with sleeping soldiers, sleeping sons, fathers and husbands, sleeping children of the War.

Somehow, during the night, two small companies of Federal and Confederate troopers had stumbled upon one another in this sylvan hollow on a Georgian farmland and fought until every last man was dead but for the solitary figure now standing swaying above them with a weapon still dangling from a bloodied hand.

Before this day he'd already seen more dead than any man should in a hundred lifetimes, yet had not heard their message until this moment where he stood trapped in time, halfway between heaven and hell.

Now the message was agonizingly plain.

In every sleeper's face he identified the common dominant expression, if not of contentment or resignation then certainly of passionate commitment. That they had died so heroically and now rested together so tranquilly told Ben Charron that every man, regardless of the colour he wore, had died for his country, unswerving in the belief that the country was worth dying for.

Dead patriots all.

It was America that was honoured in this place, not the North or the South. And in that searing moment he knew that he had been chosen to carry on the battle for America on behalf of all those who'd fallen here. Could, must, would . . .

Slowly the cornfield dimmed in his vision and he was again floating upwards through layers of grey mist towards a very different kind of light where the reality of pain, memory and a raging thirst told him he was still alive, ten years on from a Georgian cornfield, half-entombed in desert earth and rubble upon the cold stone floor of Holy Ghost Canyon. He was alive.

Charron popped a pebble into his mouth to assuage his raging thirst. Standing in a pit of black shadows staring off warily towards the right, where a shaft of dim starlight penetrated, he fingered the caked blood on the side of his head and rolled his tongue over lips that still felt thick from the dope.

He'd retched once and felt better for it. His holster was empty and he'd only given up the search for his .45 at the spot where he'd regained consciousness upon hearing what he'd thought to be whispering voices.

He knew now the voices had been the product of a combination of some knockout drug, a badly gashed head and the uneasy acoustics of Holy Ghost Canyon.

The canyon was rugged and eerily ugly, with strange wind-carved formations of rock rearing against the sky like mighty gargoyles surmounting a madman's cathedral. Isolated, ugly and inhospitable though it might be, every man who tackled the desert held it in the highest esteem, not because of what it lacked, but what it possessed.

Water.

The very word caused his tongue to swell. He tugged a battered Dollar cigar from his tattered shirt pocket, but didn't light it. Just sucked. It was deathly quiet above, but there was no way of knowing if a bunch of killers might not be lying on the rim up there, just waiting for him to make an appearance.

Muscles bunched along his jawline as he mashed his teeth down upon the stogie.

His guess was that the men he'd dimly seen and heard were Clay's Red Creek bunch. There was, however, no guesswork involved in figuring who it was who'd fooled him, doped him and damn near got him killed.

The beam of light he was looking at was strengthening. He gazed upwards, realized he could now make out the beetling cliffs whereas before all had been dark. It was time to move.

Hugging the rock wall, Charron worked his silent way through brush and rock. He had his bearings now, knew the location of the spring from which he'd filled his canteens on the journey south.

It was an hour before he dared water at the spring. All was quiet, and his strength was flooding back. Even so, it was a further two cautious hours before he stood amongst the campfire ashes staring at the crumpled wanted dodger he'd found on the rim.

It read:

WANTED
GANG KNOWN AS RED CREEK BOYS
$500 REWARD
APPLY SHERIFF REED
RIO SALTO JAIL

He began to scout. Within the hour, the sign had told him plenty. Two Mexicans riding mares had shown up first two days earlier and set up camp. They'd been joined later by another three, with the last man coming in just yesterday. The outlaws had been waiting here for Clay to arrive and Charron had delivered him right on time.

He realized just how lucky he'd been when he found the spot where he'd gone over. It was the only place in the canyon wall that was broken and degraded, a fifty-yard wide landslide of earth and broken rock sloping steeply down all the way to the floor.

The party had left in a hurry a couple of hours before first light, following the Donner Road north, so the tracks told him. He climbed atop a boulder, but saw nothing but naked desert under a strengthening sun. It was fifty miles to the next northern waterhole on the far side of the desolate sector known as The Breaks. He had neither a mount nor vessels for toting water. He sat in the shade of a rocky overhang and torched his first cigar in many hours. He then settled down to wait and see what the day might bring. The Indians had taught him patience also.

He started violently as a huge, crucifix-shaped shadow flowed silently over him then reappeared on the canyon floor far below. He jerked his head up to see the great Sonoran buzzard planing down out of the sun. He brandished his sawn-off grimly. 'Dust off, you ugly sonuva. I'm a long way from dead.'

But the scavenger wasn't interested in him. It vanished behind a bulging outcrop below and didn't reappear.

Something was dead down there. Or somebody.

CHAPTER 6

MANHUNT

The man had plummeted sixty feet from the rim on to solid rock. There was a bullet wound in his thigh and Charron figured he'd lost his balance in the darkness during the gunfight and fallen to his death.

The buzzard hadn't had time to get busy before he found the corpse.

He had no idea how long he stood there as though transfixed by the bloodied motionless figure upon the altar of stone. Just another dead man, reasoned the logical part of his mind. Something far, far more than that, countered a second inner voice. He was confused by his reaction, yet was in no shape to analyse it. With a shake of his head he got busy instead.

It was brutal work fashioning a cairn of rocks over the remains of the man known as the Dutchman. The sun was directly above and flooded the canyon with infinite fire. Still not fully recovered from the potent kick of the dope, he nonetheless laboured steadily, ignoring the way in which the heatwaves rippling up from the baking rock distorted his vision.

The body was beginning to swell before his work was completed. The prayer Charron said over the cairn, clutching his hat to his chest, was the same one he'd spoken over the dead in the Tennessee cornfield eleven years earlier.

He'd seen too many dead in his lifetime, but none had affected him so powerfully as this unknown badman, and he knew something momentous had happened to him in this strange hour, something that would change his life forever, yet he had no idea why or how.

It took an hour to climb back to the rim, by which time he was lathered with sweat and rubber-legged, yet remained alert and keen of eye.

Far out along the Donner Road northward he detected a black speck of movement, a sluggish lift of dust. He checked out the sawn-off he'd found under the corpse, idly fingering the five notches hacked roughly into the stock as he moved off to wait in the shade.

A half-hour later, he blinked and leaned forward. He saw now that it was a two-wheeled vehicle raising the dust out there, a buggy by the looks, with a leather hood, drawn by a dapple grey.

Felicity McMaster's buggy; he was ready to wager on it.

Long before the outfit drew within rifle range, he was able to confirm it was the girl playing the reins. No sign of anyone following her. He was angry, but didn't let it show, didn't speak as the grey's hoofs clattered over flinty shale with the girl leaning back on the reins finally to draw up before him.

He didn't know what he expected, but it certainly wasn't the spectacle of her springing to the ground and rushing toward him with tears in her eyes. 'Oh God! Oh, thank God, Ben, you're alive. I can't believe it.'

'I reckon that'd be the truth, at least,' he said, standing. The girl halted as the shotgun's twin muzzles yawned at her from close range. 'Close enough, Bright Eyes.' His stare was glacial. 'All right. Where is he?'

She made a vague gesture. 'Gone. They've all gone.'

'Except the one they left behind.'

'Dutchy?' Her eyes widened as they fixed on the rifle. 'That's his gun. Is he . . . was he. . . ?'

'He's dead. One of your hero's pards, I take it?' He'd had ample time to speculate at length on the events which had almost cost him his life. Also about the mistakes he'd made. No, he corrected. Mistake, singular. He'd trusted a pretty woman. One *big* mistake.

'Ben, you must try to understand. I didn't know it would turn out as it did. Please let me explain—'

'Cut it,' he said roughly, resting the butt of the dead man's weapon on the stone between his boots. 'Instead of listening to more lies, let me tell you what happened. You and Clay were lovers, like Mama's girls hinted. You were bent on setting him free anyway you might when I showed up at just the right time. First you conned me into hinting what trail I'd be taking home. Then, when we visited the telegraph office, while I was contacting

Capital City, you were firing off wires to the Red Creekers, alerting them to get ready for action, where to lay for me.'

'Please, Ben, I beg of you—'

'So they were all roosting up here at the canyon when you took me out of the game with a mug of drugged coffee. That was their cue to show themselves and finish me off, only they weren't up to the job. But you'd got what you wanted, hadn't you, Bright Eyes? Your outlaw was free, and you figured I was dead when you lit out.' He paused with a scowl. 'Only thing I don't figure is what brought you back.'

Felicity was more composed by this time. He'd assessed her as a strong woman from the outset. That strength showed now.

'Very well, Ben. I'll concede you are right. . . but only up to a point. You see, knowing Ethan was innocent, I was obliged to try and save his life. And, yes, I used you, and I'm sorry. Everything that happened up until we camped here last night was more or less exactly as you say. I hated putting that stuff I got from Mama Tonio into your drink, but it was the only way to avoid bloodshed. Or so I thought.'

'Let me guess,' he said, sarcasm roughening his tone. 'You were shocked when the party got rough, right?'

'There was to be no shooting. Ethan promised, and I believe he meant it. But when Krile saw you almost helpless, he . . . he did exactly what he did the night the gang robbed the Valdez hacienda.'

She paused to brush quickly at her eyes. Charron

studied her dispassionately.

'Spare me the crocodile tears. They don't wash. Let me guess about the Valdez killing. Clay told you Krile killed Valdez, right?'

She gestured helplessly.

'You'll never believe anything I tell you, and I don't blame you . . .'

He moved closer, menacing her with rain-coloured eyes. 'All right, dammit! Where did they go? Tell me quick and tell me straight.'

'What does it matter now?'

'Because I'm going after them!'

Her eyes widened. 'No, Ben. Good God, haven't you had enough? Look at you. They nearly killed you last night and surely would if you pursued them now. There are still four of them, you know.'

'Five,' he corrected, striding to the buggy.

'Four,' she insisted, coming to his side as he checked out the water canteens on the buggy floor. 'You see, there was a terrible quarrel up at the place they called Togan's Butte. Ethan was furious over the gunplay here and told them he was through with them all. I. . . I honestly thought he and Reuben Krile might kill one another, they were so angry. But after a long time everybody calmed down a little and agreed to part company. Ethan begged me to go with him, but then he and I quarrelled. I was horrified by what had happened here and told him I was coming back to see if you and Dutchy might still be alive.'

'Sure you did,' he grunted. He climbed up into the

rig and untied the reins, the springs compressing under his weight. The grey snorted in protest. 'Coming or staying?'

'You hate me now, don't you, Ben?'

His mouth twisted. His head ached and the heat was murderous. He was a man who made few professional errors, and wouldn't rest until he'd rectified this one.

'Last call for Togan's Butte!'

With a helpless sigh, the girl climbed up, was scarcely settled beside him when he whirled the rig around and slapped the horse into a trot; a crazy thing to do in this heat, or so she thought. But Charron was watching the sun and figuring how long it would take to reach the butte. Right now the desert was as still as death, lying stricken and comatose beneath brutal layers of heat. But when the night cold came down and the overheated air rose, the resulting night winds of the arid lands, the 'south-west mistral' as they called it, could blow all night long, sweeping up everything, erasing everything that the day had left behind.

Things like sign and tracks.

He didn't know how much of her story he believed, but this manhunter always totally trusted whatever his eyes told him. He had to reach those tracks before they vanished from sight.

The butte towered huge and mysterious in the dusty moonlight. Deep pools of black shadow were cut sharply by silvered upthrusts of granite. The Togan's Butte sector had been completely quiet and still upon their arrival, but already the sands were rustling before the errant winds as the mesquite gave up its sweet night scents.

The flare of a Vesta briefly illuminated Charron's features as he lit up his first stogie since quitting the canyon hours earlier. It had been dusk when they reached the outlaws' campsite, with sufficient daylight to afford him ample time to study every last fragment of sign.

He'd discovered the outlaws had made no attempt to conceal their tracks; why should they? So their every movement was written there in the sand, as clear and specific to the eyes of a trailsman as the headlines of the *Capital Weekly Herald*. Most surprising of all to a sceptical manhunter was the discovery that the story revealed clearly by all this undisturbed physical evidence tallied precisely with what Felicity McMaster had said about what had happened here. He'd examined two sets of tracks – those of the grulla and the horse he'd supplied Clay in Rio Salto – leading away northwards up the Donner Road, just as she'd said. He also found the spot where the four Red Creek survivors had veered away south-east into the Bleaks; Felicity said she'd heard Krile announce their intention of heading back to the familiarity of Red Creek where they planned to hole up for a spell.

It took him time to absorb the significance of all this, forcing him to review recent events. She'd made his acquaintance, won his trust, played him for a sucker with the adroitness of an Abilene table boss, doped him, damn near got him killed – yet now was seemingly playing her cards as straight and honest

92

as they were dealt from the shoe.

How did you figure?

He circled the rig in the deepening dusk, checking the horse's feet, shaking the canteens to make a fresh estimate of their contents. There was still ample supply to see two people and a horse safely out of the desert up into the rangelands of Tolorosa County, he calculated. Of course, Clay had a long lead with a solid horse underneath him, plus the grulla as a remount. Every moment of delay was extending the outlaw's lead, yet still the governor's man seemed in no great hurry as he paced to and fro, blowing fragrant gusts of blue tobacco smoke into a darkening sky and spinning a dead man's .32 Winchester by the trigger guard like it was a Colt .45.

Outwardly he didn't seem to be paying much attention to his companion, yet was aware that something was riding Felicity McMaster hard. But how to get her to reveal it? That was the trick.

Finally he grunted, 'All right, moon's up. Time we were travelling.'

'Where to, Ben?'

'North. Where else?'

No reply. She climbed up beside him, he clucked to the horse and they were underway again, a straight-backed couple sitting up just like respectable courting folk setting out for a Sunday afternoon spin around Capital City.

The wind rose and the cold bit deeper as the dreamlike landscape drifted by on either side of spinning yellow wheels, growing increasingly eerie and haunted-looking in the night.

Once or twice he spoke, but drew no reply. He didn't give a damn. Clay was his prime concern. Recapturing him and delivering him to Territory Prison meant completing the job he'd been assigned. And now, as always, the job was paramount.

The miles flowed behind them. The moon climbed high, grew bloated, seemed to smoke like the burnt-out ruin of an old summer moon, then grew pale and remote as midnight came and went.

He thought his companion was asleep as they approached a mighty slope where shards of shattered stone had been sliding down off a vast brooding mesa and piling up forever. He was mistaken. Suddenly she rested a hand on his arm and said, 'Please stop for a moment, Ben.'

'Why?'

'Will you do as I ask? I have something to tell you.'

He reined in. 'This should be good.'

'You don't seem concerned that there are no tracks here.'

'They're blown away, dammit. Come on, what is it you want to say—?'

Her face was white in the moonlight. 'Ethan didn't come north.'

'What?'

She looked away, shivered, drew her jacket tighter round her shoulders. Her profile against the backdrop of the mesa's dark bulk was perfect, and he was annoyed with himself for noticing.

'This is the most difficult thing I've ever had to do.'

Her voice was tight. She twisted her hands in her lap, looked down at them. 'What happened at the canyon made me realize I may have been wrong about Ethan. I'd always seen him as wild and exciting, but never bad. The same went for his friends, I suppose. Initially he told me they just happened to be visiting Valdez the night he was killed, and I believed him. Now he's admitted they went there to steal horses, and Valdez was killed, but not by him. And when I saw how eager Krile and the others were to kill you last night, especially Krile, I expected Ethan to show his authority far more than he did in trying to stop them. I . . . I'm so confused . . .'

She began to weep. Charron sat motionless. After a moment she sniffed and began to speak again, swiftly now as if eager to have done with it.

'Before his quarrel with Krile, Ethan and I had a long talk. He confided in me that he intended to break up with the boys then and there. Said he was terrified of hanging and was so excited to be free that he intended giving up his wild ways and to sever all links with the gang, the county, Southwest Territory. He . . . he told me he was heading for Texas to begin a new life and asked me run away with him.'

'So, how come you're here then?'

Felicity stared straight ahead.

'I considered it, I actually did. But, believe it or not, I felt terrible about you – so guilty. I told Ethan I felt I'd been used and made a fool of, and that I was turning back, going home. And, you know what he said? That maybe it was best. He doesn't care. It was then I knew I'd made the right decision.'

'Uh-huh.' He felt her words had the ring of truth. But how did you trust anyone who'd come within an ace of getting you killed? 'So Clay's struck east then . . .' He was listening to the wind and envisioning the landscape by the still light of dawn. Clean, bright – and trackless. 'Do you know which route he took?'

'What would you do if you knew?'

'Catch him and finish my job, of course.'

'Even though you at least half believe in his innocence now?'

'I just do what I'm paid for.'

'You must worship money to do such terrible work,' she said bitterly. 'Even if it is for the Governor. It's immoral. How can you live with yourself?'

'I do what I do for America.'

She stared at him, sensing his integrity. Somehow, it was what she needed to hear. The decision she'd been agonizing over suddenly seemed inevitable.

'If I should tell you where I think Ethan might be found, would you promise—?'

'No deals, Bright Eyes. I don't make deals.'

She told him anyway. She was too tired not to.

The tall man on the white horse had become a familiar sight around the little border pueblo. Every day that week he'd set off from Señora Robles' adobe on his big red horse to climb Saturnino Mesa, but had never managed to make it all the way up the final steep slope to the crest before weakness forced him back.

If Ethan Clay Should Hang

The village was sympathetic even though the Americano was solitary and stern and spent his afternoons shooting at cacti and Joshua trees in the gulch at the back of Señora Robles' house. He had been very ill, and the medic had said he was lucky to be alive, but would carry a limp for the rest of his life due to a bullet injury to the hip and another to the knee. He said the man's name was Smith, and the village girls thought him very handsome. But a sleepy pueblo such as this was rightly wary of men of this flashy breed, although the cantina owner truly appreciated the large number of silver dollars he spent on sipping whiskey until very late every night.

Today the rider paused at the foot of the last climb, then raked his horse cruelly with his spurs to succeed in finally forcing the animal all the way to the summit.

He swung down almost smoothly, and limped up and down the spine of the high point, swinging lean arms, the sun glinting from his perfectly dressed coal-black hair.

He remained there for an hour while sunrise erupted dramatically to sweep away the shadows from the broad border lands. A hundred consecutive times, his right hand blurred and whipped out the sixgun he carried in the cutaway holster riding low on his hip. He remained, he knew, as a Colt connoisseur had once described him: 'As quick as death and slick as goose grease'.

Two hours later, he kissed the widow goodbye, and as he headed north, a neighbour heard her calling tearfully, '*Adios*. Ride with God, Señor Jenner!'

He did not look back.

CHAPTER 7

GALLOWS BAIT

No desert wanderer ever came by the long-abandoned Sequoia Mine any more, and the former manager's office felt snug and secure to the freest man in the Territory. Ethan Clay sighed and waited for sleep. Too bad about Felicity. He'd given her the chance to come with him, only she'd been too concerned about the big man.

Charron!

What a loser!

Not like Ethan Clay, the big winner. So he'd miss the boys some, only natural. And he knew he loved Felicity more than he hated prison. But when you got right down to cases, all that really signified was that, come daybreak, he'd be heading directly for Texas non-stop on Charron's big blue nag – and he'd promised merciful Jesus he'd never, but never, dabble in the owlhoot again.

Drifting off fast now beneath a mouldy old Fort

Union blanket, he smiled at a final thought. In the Lone Star State he'd get them to call him Tex. Just Tex . . .

And so he slept without dreaming while that evil mistral whimpered, whispered, hissed and whined its way through what remained of the old Sequoia Mine, rattling sheets of tin, tempting shutters loose and blowing great gusts of sand and loose earth down the yawning black mouth of the dead mine where honest men had once toiled hard and long in a way he could not even imagine.

He slept like the dead for four hours straight to come awake in an instant at the cold touch of a gun muzzle pressing lightly, but firmly, against his temple.

Charron walked the streets of the Capital, killing time until he was due at the statehouse. He'd never seen this old, sun-baked city – a curious blend of the oldtime down-at-heel and boom-town get up and go – as crowded as it was this week preceding the elections. He'd always liked it insofar as it was one of those rare places where a man could find just about whatever it was he wanted, whether it be peace, anonymity, fame, excitement, riches, grinding poverty, someone to love or at least someone who'd pretend they loved you long enough for you to get your money's worth.

But Capital City had changed, and not for the better. He'd sensed this the moment he'd arrived, in the dark hour before dawn with a woman and a killer, was now even more sharply aware of just how different it was as he made his slow, deliberate way past a row of market stalls where conversations dried up at his approach and didn't resume until he was well past.

The city was a volatile mix of the old and the new, the clash of the boomtime generation with the old cultures of Mexican feudal lords with their ancient loyalties, he reflected. It was also living out the final weeks of a highly unpopular and allegedly corrupt administration, with all the tension and uncertainty that this engendered.

And somehow, in a way he still hadn't fully expected, his journey south to collect one easy, smiling bravo named Clay had exploded into something far outweighing its seeming importance.

The Governor had assigned him the job of fetching Clay back quickly, quietly and without fuss. But when his secrecy was mysteriously breached, ushering in a series of violent events that had created headlines right across the south-west, suddenly the outlaw's fate, the whole question of the man's guilt or innocence and the Governor's motives in insisting on staging the execution in the Capital, had come to dominate the entire election campaign.

For every poster advocating a vote for the Republican or Democrat ticket there were several demanding Clay be set free, or at least afforded a re-trial. Plus, of course, the ubiquitous 'Clay Must Hang' banners to be seen all over this divided city.

And somehow Ben Charron found himself elevated by many to the role of the arch villain of the piece for having hauled their unlikely hero back to the Capital despite at least two murderous attempts to prevent his doing so.

So he decided simply to relax while maintaining full alert. He watched his back and avoided dark alleyways while marvelling that Clay had assumed such importance. In his judgement, the man was a straight-out killer. Why couldn't the have-nots have chosen someone more impressive as the symbol for their struggle against the haves?

Some distance ahead the narrow street opened up to give eventually on to the central square, Federation. Fluttering Rager lamps and brass-based ground lanterns cast soft islands of light which grew stronger as night came on.

Bronzed deeply by the desert, and with only a piece of court plaster affixed to his left temple and a fading cheekbone bruise testifying to the violence he'd survived, Charron was a familiar sight to many as he entered the crowded square.

Capital City knew him as a man of the gun, but with a unique difference. Marshal Pearl's occasional special deputy troubleshooter was known as a man with an almost obsessive regard for law and order, and was generally viewed as a more committed enemy of the Territory's ungodly than even the high-powered lawmakers who frequently hired his specialized skills. He was feared and respected here; more the former than the latter since his involvement in the Clay affair, he sensed.

He reckoned he should allow for the fact that many more citizens seemed to have swung the outlaw's way based on a growing perception his trial may have been suspect, hence the hostility towards himself and the administration.

As though to confirm this impression of a city dangerously divided and politically overheated, the sudden oom-pah-pah of a tuba and the clatter of a kettle drum heralded the appearance from a side street of a rag-tag-and-bobtail procession of citizens toting hand-painted slogans clamouring for Clay's release. One daring marcher, in stained baggy linen pants, even brandished a placard that demanded:

> IMPEACH LANE NOW
> CLAY TRIAL A MISCARRIAGE
> CITIZENS UNITE!
> JOIN THE MIGUELS NOW!

He stopped and scowled. The so-called 'Miguels' were a band of ragged, militant young poor committed to the overthrow of the administration, and were responsible for much of the violence associated with Territory politics in recent times.

The noisy cavalcade attracted new marchers as it wound its way around the ornamental fountain and statue in the centre of the square, and cheering erupted from sectors of the crowd. This was immediately countered by anti-Clay factions, and several brawls erupted. Sentries at the statehouse gates jumped to full alert and deputies emerged with rifles tucked beneath their arms as the weaving snake of humanity finally came to a halt before the stone jailhouse.

If Ethan Clay Should Hang

At another time, Charron would have automatically crossed to either the jailhouse or gates to lend his presence to the authorities. He was puzzled and annoyed by his reluctance to do so tonight as one wild-eyed Miguel began to castigate loudly the city marshal regarding his notorious prisoner. Mostly Charron saw things in black and white where the law was concerned, but some half-tones appeared to have corrupted his thinking recently where Ethan Clay was in question.

'The hell with it!' he muttered, and turning his back, headed for the Welcome Hand whose smooth brandy should about set him up for supper with the élite just fine.

They would all want his full story tonight, he knew, but were due to be disappointed. He'd told Marshal Pearl everything, but it would go no further than him. As far as the unwashed hordes were concerned, he'd been jumped in Coyoteville by two killers, then crossing the desert had clashed with the Red Creek gang. No mention of the girl or the fact that Clay had actually escaped and been recaptured. The less some folks knew the better, at a time like this. He grinned with wry self-deprecation. Was he growing even more isolated and suspicious? Maybe it came with the job.

The brandy at the Hand never let you down. It was pure, strong and sociable. He wanted a second, but decided against it. A mental image of a man lying dead at his feet in the desert jolted him momentarily as he shoved the shot glass aside. What the hell had happened to him out there?

Shaking his head, he swept the bar with a final glance and walked out.

Across the plaza, the statehouse lights blazed reassuringly. Closer to hand stood the Governor's gallows surrounded by a small crowd of citizens who were predictably debating the rights and wrongs of the impending execution. The majority seemed to be against it.

Charron had his own spacious quarters attached to the army barracks. He took his time over a light second shave for the day, then climbed into the tailored black broadcloth suit they kept for him at the tailor's next door for such occasions. The boiled white shirt and string tie were his own. Dinner for him at the statehouse was always formal; suit, tie and six-gun.

And what, he found himself musing as he dressed, if Ethan Clay should hang? Would there be riots and protest marches, and blood running in the gutters as some predicted? And would the execution of one Red Creek hellion boost the Governor's flagging fortunes sufficiently to see him installed for another four-year term?

Then the big question: what interest was it all to him anyway? His part in the Clay affair was over and done with. Leastwise, he hoped so. For various reasons the whole operation had left a sour taste. He knew he needed another job right off. Something clean, straightforward and uncomplicated for preference.

Crossing the square diagonally, he angled a glance across at the long, low stone building on the southern side, facing away from the statehouse. The City Jail was squat and compact with high-barred windows, beneath which deputies with guns sagging from low-slung holsters were pacing up and down, looking edgy. Lining the flat rooftop was the row of siege cannons which, so gossip had it, the Governor had purchased from his old regiment in the event he might need them here some day.

He knew he was currently in high standing when, just halfway along the plush hallway leading to the dining rooms, with a liveried servant flanking him on either side, he was greeted personally by the great man's lady, who dismissed the flunkeys and escorted him to the dining hall herself.

'We can't begin to thank you, Mr Charron,' she gushed, a tall angular woman with handsome eyes and an impressive jewellery collection. 'I must say, when you were overdue my husband began to fear the worst. You must tell us how you managed to withstand that trouble in the desert; I'm sure it must have been terri-bly exciting.' She rested a hand on his arm and smiled coquettishly. 'But of course we were not surprised by your success. As my husband is often heard to say, "What do I need a whole army of Regulators and deputies for when I have Ben Charron?"'

This set the tone for the evening. The Lanes were effusive and flattering, Strat Dalton remote and look-ing vaguely hostile, the guest list the usual amalgam of railroad tycoons, cattle kings, meat packers, oppor-tunists, back-room boys and kingmakers.

But Marshal Pearl was the main reason Charron had accepted his invitation, and the two found the opportunity to get together after the ladies left the menfolk alone with their brandies and cigars in a large room whose walls glowed with splendid oil paintings.

Charron wanted to ask about his next job, if any, but the Washington-appointed US marshal was more interested in the job he'd just completed. Pearl was particularly interested in Jenner and Jackson and Coyoteville.

'It's plain they were hired to kill you, Ben,' he frowned. 'But by whom? Jenner was, or is, the highest-priced gun in the Territory. Clay's supporters just don't have that kind of money. Any notions who might stand to gain by forking out maybe up to two thousand dollars to have you killed and stop you completing your assignment?'

'Reckon not. But while we're speculating, I've got to tell you I had plenty of trouble with the sheriff down there. He's in the Clay camp, you know? He arrests the man, charges him with murder, then decides he's innocent after he's been found guilty. How do you figure?'

'You're not suggesting Sheriff Reed might have had something to do with those killers?'

'Likely not. But I'm next to certain it was him who spread it round I was coming for Clay . . .' He paused with a frown. 'I guess he must be certain Clay's innocent, so wanted me stopped any way he could do it.'

'Makes you wonder, doesn't it. . . ?'

'Don't tell me you're having second thoughts about that man's guilt, Marshal?'

'Why . . . have you?'

For a strange moment the two stood there just staring at one another. And Charron thought, *was* he having second thoughts? Was *this* the reason he'd not reported Felicity McMaster's actions? Had events and the time he'd spent with Clay raised the spectre of doubt about his guilt?

The marshal shook his head impatiently and spoke soberly.

'This whole thing's gone on too long, too messily. Lane has handled it badly, and now I've got a whole damned city simply fizzing with tension and at risk of erupting if anything goes wrong. Which is why I'm asking you to stay on until after it's over, Ben. Full pay, of course. It's the Governor's wish as well as mine. I know you need a break away. But as a special favour?'

He wanted to refuse. Yet there was something playing on his mind that told him he needed action now to rid him of some strange hangover from the shootout in the desert.

Before he could respond, they were rejoined by the ladies, plus one.

Felicity McMaster was stunning in a low-cut evening gown of shimmering satin with a bow at the waist, her dark hair piled high with fashionable curls framing her face.

The girl was a picture of poise as she crossed the room to take his hand and insist he dance with her and 'stop gossiping like an old fuddy-duddy'. But he sensed her tension as they turned slowly and smoothly

107

beneath a shimmering chandelier, understood the reason behind it. She'd committed a crime which could invoke the full wrath of the law. Should her actions in the desert be revealed in Charron's official report, not even all her father's money and influence could keep her out of Territory prison. She knew this. So did he.

'I submitted my report first thing this morning,' he told her casually.

Her eyes opened wide. 'Does that mean that I. . . ?'

'The only way anybody will ever know what really happened is if you tell them.'

Tears of gratitude filled her eyes and she hugged him hard, so hard in fact that the handsome couple gliding by paused curiously.

'I say, Benjamin,' the Governor said jocularly, 'would you two young folk like to be alone?'

'If they do, then we must permit it, Matherson,' his wife chimed in. 'After all, to the victor go the spoils. And Mr Charron is surely the most vaunted victor we can boast of at a time when we need all the good people we can muster if we're to succeed in our goals.'

'How right you are, my dear, how very right.' The Governor turned his head as the music ceased and he received a signal from a liveried servant framed in a doorway. 'Ah, supper time. Come along, Benjamin, I've arranged for you to sit with us.' He smiled fatuously. 'And you too, of course, Felicity. After all, I have promised your father to look after you, as I always do when you visit.'

The evening went smoothly until around midnight

108

when Charron and Dalton met by chance on the balcony. There was no love lost between the two, and a half-drunk Strat Dalton was in no mood to hide his feelings.

'Well, if it isn't the big-shot backshooter himself?' he slurred. 'What's your kill tally now, gunshark?'

'What's eating you, Dalton? Not sore because I brought Clay in alive, are you?'

Dalton paled.

'Just what do you mean by that, butcher boy? Come on, make yourself plain or by God and by Jesus I'll—'

'You'll what?' Charron drew closer. Their eyes were on a level. They'd never hit it off, never would. 'You damn near busted a gut trying to talk Lane out of bringing Clay back here to the gallows and I wonder if I'm just figuring why.' He paused then added quietly, 'Still busting to be Governor, fat man?'

Dalton dropped his glass and cocked a ham fist. He was that mad. But he didn't throw the punch, dared not. Charron nodded.

'Uh-huh, you still want it. But you're worried too, mister, worried about what I might know.'

Dalton went still. 'Meaning?'

'You didn't want me to come back with Clay on account you thought the Governor's plan to hang him here just might get him over the line. So if I'd failed, could be the party might've dumped Lane and nominated you as its candidate instead.'

'Why you . . .'

'Someone hired Jenner and Jackson to get me, deputy. Somebody with a big reason to want Clay to

109

stay where he was, and who had enough hard cash to pay for the job.'

It was a shot in the dark. Charron had no notion who'd loosed the killers on him. But the way Dalton backed away, wiping wet lips with the back of his hand, made him wonder if maybe his shot had hit the bulls-eye after all.

At that moment the string quartet struck up a dance tune and Felicity came sweeping out on to the balcony to claim him.

He didn't see Dalton again. Heading back for the barracks after midnight, after walking the girl to her lodgings, Charron had plenty to occupy his mind. Things like the question of Clay's guilt or innocence, his clash with the deputy governor, Pearl's urgent request for him to stay on until after the execution, the simmering atmosphere that enshrouded the city like a pall.

He didn't think of any of them. His mind was back in Rio Salto with someone who had no connection with any of the history-making events unfolding here. Someone, possibly the only one left, who cared for him in a way he could never allow himself to care for in return.

He toyed with the delicate figurine attached to his wristlet as he walked on by the jailhouse.

CHAPTER 8

ABILENE AGAIN

The sun, bloated and red, was rising through the vast haze left over from last night's dust storm as Sheriff Humphrey Reed came like a sleepwalker along the echoing empty street, heading for the depot where the stage from the south was due in at around seven.

The same sinister red light, tinting adobe, brick, church spire and five-pointed lawman's star alike in Rio Salto, simultaneously flooded the cluster of pock-marked hills twenty miles eastward where Red Creek had its source, and where kindling wood was always mighty scarce.

The Garcia twins cursed in both Spanish and English as they shuffled to and fro around the rocky apron in front of the cave, hungover and bad-tempered, yet watchful as always, as they gathered up sticks and dry grass for the fire.

111

They sighted the lone rider simultaneously. He was climbing towards them along the bank of the tumbling stream with the sun at his back casting his shadow hugely across the awakening land. Acting in unison as they so often did, the brothers hauled six-guns and vanished into the rocks in a second, whistling softly to alert their sleeping henchmen.

By the time the tall horseman boldly rode right up to the very edge of the apron on his black horse, just like he belonged there, he had six revolvers and one buffalo-killer of a Big Fifty rifle trained on him from cover. He couldn't see any of them, but knew they were there.

'Krile!' he hollered, his voice bouncing back off the cliffs. Calmly he crossed his slender hands on his saddle cantle waiting for a response. 'It's me! I made it!'

Reuben Krile was still knuckling sleep from his eyes. The intruder had the rising sun behind him and was surrounded by a blurring red halo. Yet the voice was familiar, so familiar in fact that the hardest of the Red Creekers wonderingly lowered his shooters as he stepped from cover.

'Jenner?' he breathed.

'Who else were you expecting? Charron maybe?'

The tall newcomer spoke like a man accustomed to being listened to, and without waiting further, pushed his flashy nag up on to the apron out of the sunrise haze, and tough Krile let out a wild rebel yell.

'Jenner!' he shouted exultantly. 'Boys, don't just stand there! Say howdy to my new buddy I told you I made down south.' Then he rushed forward to extend a hand which the rider chose to ignore as he swung his right leg over his saddle with some difficulty before stepping down and removing his splendid hat as he gazed round like a general surveying the battlefield.

Four desert-battered but wide-eyed would-be hellions stared like they were seeing a vision. In marked contrast to the Red Creekers' whipped and unwashed look, the gun king, whose striking features they'd seen staring out of the newspapers at them for years, looked as if he'd just stepped off the band box. He flicked an invisible speck of dust off his sleeve and arched an eyebrow. 'So, let me guess, Krile. Despite all your biggety talk about Clay down south, you couldn't find the guts to go after Charron after all. Right?'

Everyone began talking at once until Krile bawled for silence. It hadn't been remarkable that both he and Jenner had chosen borderland Oscura as a hideaway when the heat was on, as it was a well-known refuge to riders of the owlhoot. What had been a surprise was that the arrogant Jenner had sought him out on learning he was associated with Ethan Clay, the man whose plight had brought Jenner and Jackson to the county on a gun job that had gone all the way wrong in Coyoteville.

On hearing the Red Creekers' plans to jump Charron and free their pard, Jenner had almost begged Krile to wait until he was fit enough to join them. Time constraints made this impossible, but upon his recovery the killer had sought Krile out at the hideout he'd told him about – just in case.

113

If Ethan Clay Should Hang

Jenner showed contempt and disgust as he wolfed down a bowl of possum stew and heard about recent events along the Two Springs Trail. But having been on the trail north for two straight days, he hadn't heard about Charron delivering Clay to the Capital until now, and immediately his whole demeanour changed.

'*Amigos*,' he said, showing himself to be one of the finest-looking men in the West when he smiled, 'suddenly everything makes sense. I was meant to come here, you were meant to screw up on your big rescue caper, and Charron was meant to get to hang his hat in Capital City.' He threw long-fingered hands wide. 'It's perfect.'

Like four apprentices hanging on to the words of a master, the dangerous young men of Red Creek waited for the damaged, hate-driven killer to explain what in hell he meant.

By the time he was through, everyone was grinning as the rising sun finally lifted clear of the horizon haze to bathe simultaneously the outlaw hills and the streets of Rio Salto in golden light.

But the sheriff of Rio Salto was not smiling as he leaned the point of his shoulder against a telegraph post by the stage office and squinted out along the empty trail. What was there to smile about? He'd failed in his attempt to save the life of a man he genuinely believed to be innocent, and in so doing had compromised all the ethics he lived by. His wife was fed up with his guilt and grouchiness, he didn't sleep any more and this big, bright sun only seemed to mock him as it attempted, without success, to cajole him out of his depression.

It was with a slight start that he realized he was not alone on the landing. The man seated behind a stack of mailbags and passengers' luggage had been invisible until he leaned forward on his bench to touch a match to a freshly rolled cigarette.

Reed blinked. He'd only ever seen Doc Christian togged out in a three-piece suit once or maybe twice before. And he'd never known him to appear on the streets before the gambler's hour of noon.

Their eyes met. Reed wasn't going to speak as Christian was a testy man who was never at his best early, even if that was midday by the clock. To his surprise, the other man winked at him and gave a tough-mouthed grin, and the lawman realized he'd been drinking. Why wasn't he surprised? What he didn't figure was how come Doc was abroad all duded up and waiting at the depot.

'Leaving town?' he asked, mounting the steps. His tone was hopeful. Christian was educated, a genuine character and could be great company when in the mood. But his temperament was too uncertain to make him anything but uncomfortable to be around for any length of time.

'I guess it will break your heart, tinstar, but yes indeed, I'm heading north. All the way to the Capital, as a matter of fact.' Christian lifted his feet, examined

115

his shiny boots with satisfaction, then got up to peer along the trail. 'Yes indeed, I suspect the gory prospect of watching a sacrificial lamb offered up for the delectation of the grey masses was too strong for my feeble willpower to resist. Bet you wish you were going with me, Sheriff?'

'I thought you reckoned Clay was innocent. Like me.'

'Certainly he's innocent. Everybody knows Krile killed Valdez. But you know something, amigo, they say that innocent folks swing exactly as high as the guiltiest felon ever born.'

The man's cynical manner rang hollow to the sheriff. There was something very odd here. He was curious, but careful to employ exactly the right neutral tone as he chose his words circumspectly.

'You've always been straight with me, Doc, sometimes too straight. Why are you really going to the Capital?'

It seemed a long time before Christian deigned to reply.

'Simple. Someone asked me to go.' He grimaced. The billowing dust boiling up behind sixteen hoofs and four steel-shod wheels was rising out beyond the bridge. 'Someone pressed me to go up there and – wait for it – keep an eye out for your buddy, Charron.'

'What?'

'Oh yes, indeed. Knew that'd kick you in the *cojones*. Imagine that. Me nurse-maiding Charron. Of course . . .' His voice trailed off, then came back. 'Of course we were pards of a kind once . . . pards on the

116

rip-roaring streets of old Abilene. By God and by Judas
– those were the days . . .'

Again his words died. The stage came rolling into
the landing and for a moment everything was obscured
by dust. But the sheriff didn't seem to notice. 'Who was
it asked you to do this, Doc?'

'Friend.' Doc was curt again as he bent to pick up his
valise. 'Mutual friend of the big man and me.' He was
looking mean again. 'Hell, you don't think I'd risk my
thirsty neck in a town threatening to combust for just
anybody, do you? Now out of my way, I've got a stage to
catch.'

But Reed grabbed his arm. Suddenly days of guilt
and remorse were overwhelming the lawman. He
wanted forgiveness, needed to be shriven.

Christian stood staring at him as he babbled out
everything he insisted he tell Ben Charron when the
two met. It was a major confession to make, yet
Christian just shrugged indifferently and grunted,
'Well, that could get you jailed with any luck, amigo,'
and climbed on board.

'You promise to tell him?' Reed yelled through the
window. But Doc Christian was slumped in the far
corner, uncorking a bottle, and didn't seem to hear.
Reed was forced to step back as the driver whipped up
the team. He shook his head like a tormented beast,
wondering what had compelled him to confess that
way, yet perversely relieved that he had done so.

By the time Rio Salto had vanished behind them in
the dust, Doc Christian and his fellow passengers had

adjusted to the Concord's well-sprung rhythm. Five miles out, on a clear blue morning, he peered from his window to see a slowly moving cloud of hoof-lifted dust rising to the north. Cross-country riders travelling pretty fast northward out Red Creek way, by the looks.

'Evening, Mr Charron.'

'Deputy.'

'What's happenin' on the streets, sir? I've had to send out five squads to separate disturbances since sundown.'

'Big trouble building, I'm afraid. They've heard about the bench's decision not to allow a motion of appeal put forward by Miss McMaster's attorneys on Clay's behalf. The troublemakers have been waiting for something like this to set the flint to the tinder. How's the prisoner?'

'Doin' fine, I guess. Say, I just brewed up. Would you say no to a mug of coffee first?'

'Why not?'

Twenty feet away in his ten-by-eight cell, Ethan Clay heard every word from the front office, every creak of a chair. And from the near distance came the urgent, erratic sounds of restive horses and running feet, of angry shouting interrupted sporadically by the sudden clash and clatter of violence.

The territorial capital was teetering on the brink of a riot tonight, and all because of him.

He raised his head. Glints of light flickered in black curls. Outside, a summer night wind blew and he remembered such nights when he and Felicity had galloped across the endless acres of the McMaster ranch on half-broken mustangs and it felt as though he'd be young forever.

But they were going to kill him after all.

The mobs might riot, and maybe his boys would try something again yet, although he doubted it, for they'd never really been friends, just hangers-on. He knew his last hope had been the appeal, and now the relentless machine of the law would roll over him and grind him into the dust.

Scared? Sure he was. But with luck he might die without them knowing it.

'On your feet in there!'

He turned lazily and stared at the lock-up insolently. The lock-up's mongrel dog bared its yellow teeth at him. It was trained to hate all the prisoners.

'You got a visitor, world-beater. Better spruce yourself up.'

'*Amigo*, if I slept with hogs for a week and had double smallpox, I'd still look better than you on the best day you ever lived.'

'Why, you dirty little tinhorn—'

'Get out,' a deep voice interrupted. The lock-up turned to find Charron filling the doorway with his wide-shouldered bulk. The man ducked his head and left, the dog dragging its tail.

'You know, big man, some men have got it and some just wish they did. I guess you've got it. Authority, that is. At least, you scared me and that hound dog.'

119

If Ethan Clay Should Hang

Charron came and stood before the barred door. He wore a leather hip jacket and carried a shotgun in his left hand. His knuckles were skinned and bruising showed down one side of his jaw. Every available man was out on the streets tonight as buildings caught fire, riots erupted and the portents of real trouble continued to make themselves felt. Seemed every Clay supporter in the city had convinced himself that the appeal before the bench of District Court 31 would bring down a finding of sufficient inconsistencies and aberrations about his trial in Rio Salto to warrant a stay of execution and a full judicial revision of the case. This was now one angry town.

'I'm sorry, Clay. About the way things turned out.'

'Don't hand me that, Charron. You took every cent of their dirty money to do a dirty job, and Lane and his whole bunch of crooks are pinning your picture up on their walls right now. I can take that. I'm tougher than you think. But don't give me that sorry gaff. You gotta be human to be sorry.'

Charron cocked his head. Sounded like a heavy wagon tipping over across the square. Shouting rose then faded, followed by three evenly spaced shots. Warning fire.

'You're right about one thing. You *are* tougher than I thought. Anything you want?'

Clay went to the door and grabbed the bars, staring at him from close quarters.

'Just one thing I want, big man, and I'm getting it. A close-up look at the biggest phoney that ever walked.

120

That's you, hero. You make out you're so fine and right-
eous while you go round stockin' boothills all over the
Territory. But all you are is a cold-blooded killer with a
heart you could fit into a hole in a tooth. Maybe I'm no
good, but I'll never be some kind of murder machine,
like you.'

He stepped back and jerked a thumb.

'OK, you gave me what I wanted. Vamoose. Go kiss
Lane's ass. And pray real folks never find out just what
you really are.'

Charron nodded and left. The lock-up and two
deputies glanced up as he entered the front office.
They'd heard every word. He was unfazed – or so he
wanted to believe. Yet, taking down his hat, he turned
to glance back through the archway and, for a fleeting
moment, an expression of naked regret ravaged his
features. Then he clapped the Stetson to his head and
went striding out in response to a drunken voice bawl-
ing, 'All right, lawdogs, wheel out your big bad
gunslinger and I'll show you the colour of his yellow
guts!'

Capital City's worst night was underway.

Down by the river on the north side, the adobes gave
way to a straggle of hovel-lined alleys and broken-down
shacks. The cantina, as was usual these nights, was
crowded and the mood was turning ugly. There was too
much whiskey and tequila mixed with too much talk
about elections, hangings and, as always, the widening
gap between rich and poor, powerful and helpless.

If Ethan Clay Should Hang

Someone threw a bottle, and a window went out with a crash. Surging packs of brawlers came together and a flimsy wall went down beneath their weight. A half-naked woman ran screaming from a side door, and a bearded man wielding a slat with a nail in was beating up a newspaper reporter from across the border when five mounted Rangers, two deputies and Ben Charron rode up to the front gallery.

Peace was quickly restored with gun barrel, club and billy stick. But before the peacemakers could leave, the glow of flames back on the square warned that the real trouble was just beginning.

Charron stopped off at The Bar With No Name for a shot. The fire some fool had lit at the library had been doused, but the burnt stink was everywhere, in the air, in his throat. But brandy took care of the latter, and he was toying with the idea of ordering another when an old man shuffled up to him, sucking on the tobacco-stained corners of a ragged moustache.

'Seems to me you're looking pretty chipper for a feller that's been having a mighty busy night, Mr Charron.'

'Beer or brandy?' Charron responded. The old man was both a drunk and a sometime informant. But Charron wasn't in the mood for company tonight.

'Well, mighty kind of you, sir. Guess I'll have a shot of rye, huh?'

Charron rolled a coin on to the bartop, was about to leave when the man tugged at his sleeve.

'Hey, you don't believe it, do you, Mr Charron?'

'Huh? Believe what?'

'That the kid's guilty.'

'I don't want to talk about that. Neither should you, pops. There's been too much talk already—'

'Omar.'

'Huh?'

'You know. The bench judge what sat on Clay's trial. Omar Burlinson.'

Charron's eyes narrowed. 'What about him?'

'Drinks even more than I do these days, Mr Deputy, sir. I ought to know on account he lives right by me on Antelope.'

'Meaning?'

'Could be his conscience troublin' him, if you ask me. Mebbe somethin' he done that was real bad – if you get my meanin'.' And tapping the side of his nose with a bony forefinger, the old man slunk away as though suddenly afraid he'd said too much.

Charron scowled after him. It was two in the morning, yet the square was still restless and noisy. He could almost feel the hostility and defiance crackling in the air. Hostility, defiance, fear, suspicion, resentment – all the indicators of open rebellion, but not that yet.

He looked for the old bum, but couldn't see him. His throat was dry again. Then he realized it was a new day and his three-shot limit was untouched.

He clicked his fingers for another brandy, was taking his first sip when he heard the batwings creak and the sound of a familiar shout.

123

'Abilene all over again, by God!'

Charron turned. He was the only man in that bar-room who knew the significance of those words. Doc Christian stood beneath the sallow yellow lamps with his hard-hitter hat tilted over one eye, a short cigar stuck between clenched teeth and the studded thorn-wood grip of a Pony Express revolver visible beneath his coat, looking every inch like a man raring for action.

'Well, aren't you even going to offer a traveller a greeting, Charron?'

Charron's jaws clamped tight. If there was one commodity the Capital had in profusion tonight, it was trouble, and he thought he'd at least left this particu-lar brand of trouble safely behind in Rio Salto.

'What are you doing up here, Christian?'

'Do you hear that?' The newcomer invited the drinkers to witness the discourtesy. 'An old wartime buddy rides a stage without springs a hundred miles to help out another old wartime buddy, and what does he get? Gratitude? Appreciation? A drink, even? Forget it. But then, that's Mr Charron, as I'm sure you all know only too well.'

'You're drunk, Doc,' he said quietly as the other crossed to the bar to dump his valise by the foot rail.

'Half-drunk. Big difference. Bartender, pour me something that'll take the sour taste of inhospitable-ness out of me.'

The drink hit the bar and Charron watched the Doc go to work on it in silence. He knew this man only too

124

well. His showing up here this way was no accident. Doc would explain in his own time – and it had better be good. He had problems enough without this man adding to them.

By now, almost everyone had lost interest in the newcomer, although a few who knew Christian continued to glance his way curiously from time to time. There were many new faces in the troubled city right now, and those who knew Doc's reputation were speculating on whether someone might have hired him and his gun in the event of matters getting out of hand.

Christian smacked his lips as he lowered his empty glass. 'Well?' His tone was brusque now.

'Well what?'

'You're itching to know why I'm here.'

'I could care less, Doc.'

'Reckon she figured you'd say that.'

'She? What are you talking about?'

Christian met his eye squarely and something seemed to twist inside him like a wrench forcing a rusty bolt. 'Terasina, of course. She made me follow you up here to look out for you. For old times' sake, as she put it. Imagine that, big man. Like I said, Abilene all over. Only thing, we were pards then. What are we now?'

'I don't believe you.'

Doc's face was hard.

'Why not? I never lied to you. Never double-crossed you with a woman either, as I recall.'

Charron refused to rise to this bait. Christian was

here and he needed him. It was at once galling and reassuring to know that there was probably nobody he'd rather have at his side over the next twenty-four hours than this feisty, prickly, unpredictable man standing before him.

'He'll have another,' he told the bartender.

'I buy my own,' Christian said, snapping down a coin.

'Suit yourself.'

'Mud in your eye.'

Christian gulped the raw spirits down and fixed him with a strange stare. 'What?' Charron challenged. The Doc sniffed and took out his tobacco. 'When did it happen?' he demanded, rolling a cigarette one-handed.

'What are you talking about?'

Doc's face disappeared behind a cloud of smoke. 'When you hung up your shooters, of course. When? How?'

Anger shadowed his rain-coloured eyes. He was doubly angry because the other had gleaned his secret when he'd been certain it was hidden deep. How could the lousy little scut know?

'I don't know what the hell you're talking about.'

Doc leaned his back against the bar and gazed out of the louvred doors. He sighed heavily as though burdened.

'It never happens to men like me. We shoot people for the same reason we drink. We don't give a damn. But the geezers with a mission – and you'd be the biggest fool missioner I ever heard of – you care too

126

freaking much, so that it grinds you away bit by bit until one day something snaps and you can't do it any more.' He turned his head to study him. 'So, how did it happen?'

Charron's iron face was grey. He stared at the man, but saw instead a body with his bullets in him lying on the bloodied floor of Holy Ghost Canyon. A Red Creek hellion who meant nothing to him, killed in a messy shootout, had affected him as had no other. He had a crazy feeling he couldn't use a gun again, but meant to get over it without anyone even suspecting it. Christian didn't suspect, he knew.

'You're drunk and you're a damn fool, Doc.'

'Well, you'll tell old Doc eventually – if you live. Lucky she sent me to wet-nurse you, huh? Oh, before I go, did I tell you about Reed?'

'What about him?' Charron was happy to change the subject.

'It was him who spilled the word you were coming to get the kid,' Christian replied, going out. 'Said he did it because he wanted someone to stop you taking an innocent man away to die. What's the world coming to?'

CHAPTER 9

RAGING NIGHT

It seemed the sun would never set on a day much like the one before, only worse in every regard. More tension, more clashes between the factions, more lawmen on the streets and far more drinking in bars and cantinas than would have been good for any city anyplace, much less one teetering on a knife edge.

Yet while men like Ben Charron and the deputies broke up brawls, closed down the worst dives and reassured the citizens on Federation Square that everything was well in hand, the young impoverished gangs of the city's north side, the so-called Miguels, simply couldn't wait for nightfall to come down upon a day that had brought them such huge and unexpected support. The members of this most militant of the pro-Clay, anti-government factions still found it hard to believe their eyes as they played host to the four gunslung newcomers gathered before them in an old mill half-concealed by a strip of shadowed woods on the fringe of Losertown.

Sure, everyone knew the Red Creek bunch were Ethan's good pards. But who'd ever have guessed the bunch would have the nerve to show up here to help bust him out?

Yet, at Krile's address, continued unease began to taint the gaunt young faces of his audience. They were all geared up for action tonight, yet it was beginning to sound, from the way the husky Red Creeker was proposing they bust Clay out of the lock-up, that a man could get killed real easy.

Krile sensed them weakening and didn't try to conceal his disgust. The hard man and new boss of the bunch held the city breed in contempt. All the bunch did. But the simple fact was that they needed the support of every hothead they could muster, needed every man they could get. Luckily they had an ace up their sleeves.

The Miguels had no notion what the Creekers were about when they were invited to step outside. There was smoke in the air from the riot fires and it was several minutes before anything happened; the gang was playing its dramatic moment for all it was worth.

He rode down slowly from the trees, silhouetted against the starlight. As he drew closer, it was seen he was tall and well-made with wide shoulders and narrow hips. But it wasn't until he reined in and

129

fingered back his hat to reveal a gauntly handsome face that Slinger Dunne's cousin gasped in recognition.

'Judas Priest,' he breathed. 'We heard you was dead, Mr Jenner. Hey, Slinger, does this mean—?'

'It means, mister,' the horseman cut in coldly, 'I've come to this pesthole to set a good man free. Not only that, amigos, but we're taking out the high-stepping bastards that helped put Ethan Clay in the death cell and have been riding roughshod over you all this week.' His voice lifted. 'I mean the dog sheriff, Pearl – and the marshal's stinking running dogs, Christian and Charron. They're going to die tonight – I swear it on this!'

His right hand blurred and an American Colt revolver filled his fist, swifter than a striking adder. It was deliberately theatrical, but effective. By the time he'd slipped the weapon away, Jenner knew he had every man Jack of them, that his long-awaited hour of revenge was at hand.

The rusted iron roof of the Capital City Salvation Hall reverberated to angry shouts from within. A fat man punctuated the speeches with weighty blows on a muffled drum. The combination of sounds brought little flakes of rust down on the heads of the assembled. They didn't notice. This was an important meeting, so engrossing that nobody was aware of the two men who appeared silently in the doorway.

'It's up to us folk of the Legion of Decency to engage with those who would dare, with might and spite, to see this place deny justice and buy that murdering scoundrel a reprieve!'

The speaker paused to dab at his sweating brow, the big drum thudded and the two men in the doorway disappeared.

'Guess they're harmless,' grunted Doc Christian, hitching at his shellbelt. 'It's the ones that want to set him loose we'd better keep an eye on tonight.'

Charron nodded and they set off along a dark and winding street where some of the best houses in the city sat back in dignified aloofness, like grand duchesses sniffing disdainfully above a night of noises and alarums.

The pair covered half a block in silence. Christian smoked a cigarette. Both cocked their heads at a rattle of distant gunfire.

The night smelt bad, looked bad, was bad. Yet, despite this, neither man doubted his ability to execute the plan they'd hatched together with Marshal Pearl to spirit Clay away from the jailhouse and hold him at a secret destination until hanging time the day after tomorrow.

They were passing a gloomy house with a paved driveway when Charron halted to study the street number. Thirty-three. He snapped his fingers, remembering the informer at the Bar With No Name. This was the residence of Bench Judge Omar Burlinson, the man who'd presided over the Clay trial in Rio Salto. A man of distinction, rumoured to be drinking himself to death for reasons Charron could only assess as suspicious.

Time was at a premium, yet minutes later Doc Christian found himself accompanying Charron up the pathway to the good judge's door. The way Doc looked at it, if Charron hoped to crack a boozy old benchman for the good of the 'cause', he was happy to help him do it.

They rang the bell-pull and eventually a liquored-up old man answered the door and found himself virtually obliged to invite his visitors inside.

Despite failing health, a bellyful of booze and a deep fear of what the night might bring, throughout the next twenty minutes of tough interrogation concerning his handling of the Clay trial, Judge Burlinson showed no sign of telling them one damn thing – until Charron left the battered old room briefly to check on a sudden disturbance out on the street.

The muffled roar of a revolver saw him spin on his heels to go rushing back to the parlour. He slid to a halt when he saw the judge slumped back in his chair, a bullet hole in it, clutching his heart. Christian stood beneath the drop light with a smoking gun in his fist.

'What the hell—?' Charron began, but the judge's high quavering voice drowned him out.

'Don't let that barbarian kill me, Charron! I'd have told you what you want to know without coercion anyway. I wish to lay my burden down. It's been driving me crazy. All I do is drink and fret, fret and drink—'

Christian pointed the gun at the man. 'What you're saying, Judge, is that the Governor briefed you to convict Clay any which way you could. And you did it. Right?'

The once-pompous old man looked pitifully up at Charron. 'I needed the money, Charron. You don't know what it's like to be old and vulnerable. He threatened to cancel my pension . . .'

Staring down, Charron felt his anger fade. For excessive though Christian's methods may have been, they almost certainly justified the results. At last they finally knew the truth. A heinous crime had been committed, not by Ethan Clay but rather by the Governor of Southwest Territory. Seemed Felicity's suspicions had been on target after all.

'Let's hustle!' he barked abruptly, reaching for his hat. 'If that mob lynches an innocent man, we'll have the Federals on our necks, pronto.'

'Not our necks,' Doc corrected. 'Governor Lane's.'

The lethal little man was bristling with energy in stark contrast to his air of bitter lethargy and boozed-up hostility down in Rio Salto.

He holstered his gun and stabbed a forefinger at the ceiling. 'Shift Clay out of harm's way then lower the boom on Matherson Lane, all in one night. How's that for a programme, town-tamer? You know, I'm getting to appreciate the fact that Terasina sent me off here to wet-nurse you after all. This beats drinking yourself to death any day of the week.'

They hit the street together. Some distance ahead could be seen a mob jogging towards the centre of town. Several carried blazing torches which threw showers of sparks and cast their shadows hugely across the faces of flanking buildings, huge and menacing. They were yelling hoarsely and it was growing increasingly plain that some incomprehensible herd instinct had determined that tonight, not execution day, was to become the hour of resolution.

Damned fools!

They passed a row of dwellings where pale faces pressed against windows, staring out, either lusting for violence or cringing in anxiety. The closer they drew to the square, the more aware both men became of the palpable unease in the air that felt like electricity running ahead of a thunderstorm. Excitement, rumour, hostility, and too many people on the streets. All the indicators of trouble, but not quite violent yet.

Doc Christian felt it all made for an interesting night; Charron was ruthlessly intent on seeing that nothing got out of hand.

They were forced to halt at a road junction as a coach and six came sweeping by with pale-faced passengers peering out at the strange streets, wondering what was going on.

It was as the stage vanished with a clash of iron-rimmed wheels that Charron heard the first faint stutter of a kettle drum punctuated by a wild rebel yell. They hurried on for half a block farther with the sounds growing louder, then halted directly outside the swinging batwings of the Days of Glory Saloon.

Directly ahead, a phalanx of marchers had erupted from a side street, yelling and singing and waving their hats, with a pickup band of boozy musicians following hard behind, their instruments glinting in the lamp-light. Like the much smaller group they'd been tailing, these marchers toted torches and lanterns, but most favoured staves and fence slats. No guns were on open display as yet, though many men were armed.

The two men traded glances when several marchers in the vanguard unfurled a crudely lettered sign proclaiming:

NO ROPE FOR ETHAN CLAY

'Told you he was popular,' Christian remarked.

'They don't give a rap about Clay,' countered Charron. He knew the city well and clearly identified several known troublemakers in the ranks of the protesters. 'All this is just an excuse for scum to behave like scum.'

Christian took a quick pull on a metal flask and threw a mock salute.

'Whatever you say, ex-crusader. So, what's our battle plan?'

'We reconnoitre before we do anything, is what.'

'Sir!'

Charron led the way for two blocks further by which time they were within gunshot distance of the square. Here they cut into a high-walled alleyway where broken glass crunched underfoot. Suspicious of major trouble before, he felt the knot of uncertainty twist his guts as they mounted the steep iron fire stairs leading to the broad flat roof of the City Feed and Grain Barn, from which vantage point they had all of Federation Square spread out like a map below them.

'Goddamn!'

The exclamation escaped from beneath Doc Christian's moustache as they stared down.

The sprawling square was far more crowded than they'd seen it during their two-man support for Pearl's law enforcement programme in this, the week of Clay's scheduled execution.

Although there was almost a superficially festive air, with people swaggering in and out of cantinas and hotels, several big braziers burning merrily out in the centre and large numbers of citizens obviously simply out to enjoy themselves on an exciting evening, there was a sinister pulsebeat underscoring the whole surging scene.

On the far side, the statehouse stood brilliantly lit and the guards on the big metal gates had been doubled or even trebled. Small groups of deputies, Rangers and troopers could be spotted moving through the crowds, while out in the middle, large groups of pro- and anti-hanging protesters were swigging from bottles as they traded slogans and insults.

Now moving into the throng like a fiery snake directly below the barn were the torch-bearing marchers they'd followed down Mesa Vista Avenue. A store window caved in with a splintering crash and someone fired a bullet into the sky. Immediately a bunch of men began fighting on a hotel porch and a woman screamed.

136

Christian, who'd maintained an air of amused and lofty cynicism up until this moment, was finally sober.

'Not a good night to be out shopping for a pair of skivvies, eh, big man. . . ? What do you make of it? Abilene chapter two, huh?'

Charron nodded. It was an apt analogy. Abilene Two.

'Guess we'd better reconsider our plan for slipping Clay out of there now,' Christian opined. He nodded towards the jailhouse on the far side where armed men were to be seen perched up on the roof between the cannons. 'Maybe we'd do better by leaving him right where he is and you and me boosting the defence on the square proper?'

'No way.' Charron was staring down at the gallows. 'We're still shifting him to safety.'

'Have we got the authority to do that? I mean, what if the law's got other ideas?'

Charron's face resembled beaten bronze in the glow of the lights. 'I told you already, it's my personal responsibility to get that man out of there. But there's no cause for you to risk your neck too.'

The Doc sighed. 'How wrong can you be? Well, what are we waiting for?'

The flustered *teniente* was adamant. 'I cannot release the prisoner without authorization, Señor Charron. You know that.'

'All by the book, you mean?' Charron gestured towards the front. 'Listen to that mob. Are they worried about the book? The hell they are. Look, I brought him

137

in and I'm responsible for his safety. I'm escorting Clay to a safe place, *señor.*'

'Please listen to him, *Teniente,*' begged Felicity McMaster, who'd been constantly at the prisoner's side throughout the long day. 'We must—'

She broke off at the groaning, splintering crash of a door caving in close by. A deputy posted out front fired warning shots into the air and the rumbling voices of the mob turned feral and menacing.

Then from the cell block came the sound of a harmonica wailing soulfully, causing Doc Christian to grin. 'You have to hand it to that pilgrim, big man. Small wonder he rates so high with the peasantry.' He scratched his head ruefully as a dissenting voice bellowed, 'Let's bust him out and string up that damned butcher right now!' Doc sighed. 'With some, leastways.'

Charron wasn't listening. Fists were crashing on the sturdy rear door. His .45 was in his hand as he shouldered a sweating deputy aside and went to check. Reefing the door open, he lowered the piece sharply as a flushed and dishevelled Marshal Pearl entered, followed closely by Strat Dalton.

The marshal had come direct from the statehouse where, he reported, security remained strong and morale reasonably high. But, like Charron, he was now deeply concerned about the situation at the jailhouse and the safety of the prisoner. Somehow, Ethan Clay had become the focal point of the contesting political factions, and as Pearl had been in the city during the previous election he was able to make a comparison and see clearly that what was happening tonight was something more threatening than simply a boisterous case of Republican versus Democrat.

'I'm glad I found you here, Ben. You also, Mr Christian,' he added grudgingly as he fingered a drape back to study the situation out front.

He saw a sea of sweating faces bathed in angry torchlight. He swallowed hard. Tonight, some germ of hidden madness had been coaxed into healthy, shambling life by outsiders and agitators. It showed in the wild-eyed face of a logger climbing atop a wagon waving a blazing brand, it was there in a score of faces with mad eyes and cruel, wet lips. It was the face of the mob, one of the ugliest sights on earth.

He stepped back, breathing hard.

'I reckon we three can spirit our man out by the back alleys and either get him out of town or at least up to the statehouse. After that we'll clear the square and—'

'You wouldn't stand a chance,' Dalton cut in. The deputy governor was sweating afresh. He started as a rifle cracked viciously out on the square. The whites of his eyes showed as he rolled them at Charron. 'This whole freaking city's going to go up tonight if we don't give them what they want . . . and what they want is that murdering goddamn outlaw.'

'Shut it!' Charron radiated implacable authority. His hands were empty at the moment yet every man present responded to the power of his personality.

139

There was a hushed quiet as he nodded curtly to the *teniente*. 'Release Clay. The marshal and I will take full responsibility.'

'That's not a request, it's an order, *Teniente*,' Pearl supported. 'Move!'

It went quickly from there, and, within a minute, a grinning Clay was standing by the opened rear door with his hand on a pale-faced Felicity's shoulder while Charron, Christian and Pearl made their last minute plans for the breakout. But time was rushing by like a maniac with a knife. Suddenly the ceiling trembled to the sounds of violence above and, moments later, a body plummeted into the laneway from the roof. Charron took one long stride for the door then whirled round as a wild chorus of shouts and the rumble of metal on wood from out front prefaced a splintering crash, the sound of a drum of metal offcuts being rolled violently into the front doors.

Hinges burst and flying screws peppered the room as door panels caved inwards to give the defenders a chilling glimpse of the surging mob beneath the smoking lights of the square.

A deputy, reeling back from the half-collapsed doors, clutching a bloodied cheek, lifted his hoarse voice above the clamour. 'Sheriff, it's them Red Creek bastards whippin' 'em up – I just seen one of 'em. Looks like they're comin' in after their pard.'

As Pearl and Doc rushed forward, Charron shot a hard glance over his shoulder at Clay. The man was pale.

'I ain't involved,' he protested. He took a pace

forward as the building shook to the reverberations of violence, and grabbed Charron by the arm. 'The boys . . . they sneaked a message through to me that they were fixin' to bust me tonight. But I thought it was just biggety talk, and anyway, I didn't think they could do it. Guess I should've told you about it, huh?'

Charron swore and swung away to join Doc and Pearl who now stood shoulder to shoulder slamming pistoning rifle butts through the gaping rents in the doors to batter the handful of wild-eyed rioters who'd gotten past the deputies to hurl themselves repeatedly against the façade like men in a frenzy.

Something or someone had worked this mob up into a fine pitch and no mistake.

'We're dead meat if we stay put!' Christian yelled excitedly. 'It's attack or go down. Right, big man?'

'Right!'

Charron's response was instantaneous. 'Flying wedge, Marshal – you, me and Doc.' He turned. 'You deputies will follow us out and no man will take a backward step. Just have confidence. Doc and I have done this before and it works. Doc, take out the crossbar!'

Doc Christian did as he was told. The crossbar dropped to the floor with a thud and the doors began to crumple inward under the combined weight of the attackers. Then Charron lunged through what remained of the doors like a juggernaut, six-gun barrels slashing left and right too fast to follow, smashing heads and faces and powering his way through out of the office into the open air in an awesome exhibition of strength and determination.

Pearl and Christian surged after him. A burly figure swinging a carbine came at Charron, who identified Reuben Krile from his memory file a split second before sinking his knee into the Red Creeker's groin with a sickening force, then he laid a man's forehead open to the inner bone with a brutal smash of his gunbarrel which the troublemaker's grandfather must have felt from deep in his grave.

As the man went down in the wreckage, a hawk-faced figure bobbed up behind him brandishing a long-barrelled Peacemaker. It was another Red Creeker making his big play. Lips snarling and teeth bared, he loosed a wild shot that burst a lamp and knocked a picture from the wall behind.

Doc Christian shot Slinger Dunne square between the eyes.

Charron experienced a strange sensation as he watched the badman vanish under a sea of thrashing legs. He'd had ample opportunity to blow Dunne away. He should have done. He hadn't. It was eerie. With an effort of will he pulled himself together and proceeded to pump a volley of shots inches above the heads of the now faltering mob, which saw them first halt then begin to roll back as they realized two of their Red Creek allies were suddenly out of it.

Beckoning Christian and Pearl to form up with him, Charron led the way forward.

The three crossed the wide gallery in a lethal triangle formation, cutting left and right with slashing pistol blows, and now the rioters seemed to panic as they witnessed their henchmen tumbling like ninepins before this whirlwind assault.

'It's Abilene again, big man!' Doc Christian roared above the chaos, and Charron glimpsed the man's face alive with a kind of ecstasy as he broke a cowboy's ugly face apart with the heavy metal butt of his revolver, then kicked him on the way down. 'Only better!'

The flying wedge technique was something Charron and Christian had first perfected in cowboy-infested Abilene, and which they'd demonstrated several times here over recent days when situations threatened to get out of hand. It had worked then and was working again now with its old efficacy as they took the fight out and away from the jailhouse itself. With the towering figure of Charron at its cutting edge, the human juggernaut proceeded to slice into the faltering ranks of hardcases, miners, Mexicans and howling drunks like a knife splitting its way through a pine board.

Torchlight glimmered on the barrels of his sixguns as he swung them left and right like scimitars.

A manic-eyed rioter clutching a huge, hide-handled skinning knife two feet long surged to within inches of him. Christian's Pony Express six-gun yammered loud and the man dropped to the floor to be trampled by retreating boots.

'Easy!' Christian exulted, and in that moment a chilling understanding hit Charron with the speed of a flung dagger.

Too easy!

His momentum faltered. There were three rioters before him and they were running backwards even though they hadn't been touched. The eyes of two of them were focused on a spot somewhere above his head where the smoke wisped wildly in writhing tendrils as though in some kind of evil ecstasy.

He halted, and Pearl crashed into him with a curse. He didn't feel it as he jerked up his head, his eyes stretching wide as he saw the silhouette of a line of gun-toting figures dominated by a theatrically tall figure all in white getting ready to open up.

On them.

And they weren't deputies.

He was aware of two things in that shaved tip of a split-second before he could get his voice working: the entire attack on the jailhouse was a cleverly planned ambush stratagem to lure them out of the jailhouse into the open, and that instantly recognizable figure in white with a glinting nickle-plated revolver in each fist was Harlan Jenner, last seen going down under his flaming guns in Coyoteville.

'Ambush!'

Charron's bull cry lifted above the chaos just before the roof guns began to roar. In the same instant a deputy passed before him and Charron heard the rifle bullet smash the man's skull, driving the already dead body into him with such force as to bring both men to the ground.

As he hit the stones he heard the distinctive clam-

144

our of Doc's Pony Express six-shooters opening up like a Gatling, heard the screams as his lead found targets.

He heaved the dead weight off him and jumped back to his feet, guns in his fists yet not firing, even as men tumbled around him. Somehow his trigger fingers seemed frozen – a blurred image of the dead man in Holy Ghost Canyon flashed before his eyes. Muffling a curse, he saw a ducking Doc lower hot and empty guns. 'Here!' he shouted and flipped his guns in a low arc. Doc dropped his irons and grabbed the fully loaded pair out of the air and, a moment later, Christian was using them in the most lethal display of gunskill Charron had ever seen.

A sniper clutching his guts stumbled over a roof cannon then pitched head-first to the paving stones with a thud like dead meat.

Then, 'That's Jenner!' Pearl shouted, and the next moment he was reeling backwards, wounded, his face a sudden awful white as the tall, lean silhouette on the roof gunned him down.

Charron went diving for Pearl's dropped shooters with ricochets snarling all about his big figure. The Doc's .45s roared like the hammers of hell. Charron powered to his feet, his face shining with sweat, only to realize that suddenly, as though someone had thrown a switch, Federation Square had grown almost quiet. The battle was virtually over.

He looked up. The only movement on the roof now was a figure writhing in agony. It wasn't Jenner. With a curse he shouldered his way through wounded and injured fighters to go storming down the alleyway separating the jailhouse from the saddlery. Men milling about in the dim alleys behind were hurled aside by the huge, crazy-looking man in brown as he flung himself at the rusted iron ladder and seemed to go up without actually touching the rungs.

Jenner wasn't there. He wasn't to be found then or later. The silence was eerie.

Next moment a panting, bleeding Christian was at Charron's side, his teeth locked in a murderous grin. 'Time to Abilene 'em, big man. That is, unless you've lost your taste for this dirty business.'

Charron knew the man was referring to his failure to deal with Jenner. Their eyes locked momentarily, but Charron offered no word of excuse or explanation, mainly because he didn't understand his actions himself even if know-all Doc thought he had the answer.

Instead Charron pivoted to face the still dangerous square. 'All right, this square is off limits to everybody!' he roared, then charged a husky waddy in a red shirt who looked ready to dispute his ruling. Again a flashing gunbarrel winked in the evil light. The cowboy fell beneath his blow as though dead. For several thunderous moments the square rocked deafeningly as Doc Christian emptied a gunful of shots at the feet of a bunch of stragglers not fleeing fast enough for his taste.

Within minutes it was all over. From the moment a mob first gives ground it is doomed. Any mob. Charron

146

and Christian knew this better than just about anyone, and their experience was never shown to better effect than in the brief minutes that followed. They seemed to know exactly whom to pursue, whom to let run. The slightest hint of tardiness or defiance would bring a man to the spot in the blink of an eye, and someone else would hit the paving stones of Federation Square like dead meat.

Until the only men left on their feet in all of Federation Square were the battered, but broadly grinning, men under the command of the US Marshal.

'I'd heard about what happened in Abilene,' Pearl panted painfully, 'but surely this was much worse?'

'I guess mobs are about the same all over,' Charron replied, calmly refilling his Colts from his shellbelt and glancing across at the jailhouse.

'That big feller's right you know,' Doc Christian confided later to the roomful of battered and bleeding men seeking attention at the overcrowded surgery of the county hospital, just off the square. He winked at the pretty nurse as he rolled up his sleeve to display a bullet-gashed forearm. 'About mobs, that is. I can honestly claim I never met a mob I didn't hate.'

CHAPTER 10

MAN WITHOUT A STAR

'As I recall,' Doc Christian said acerbically, 'it was Aristotle, or possibly Plato, who first made the profound statement – "There's nothing as washed-up as a washed-up guntipper." You must have heard that quoted somewhere before today, big man.'

There was no reply from the man at his side at the depot on this, the first rainy day of the season with just a hint of autumn in the air.

The horses had been backed into the shafts of the big blue Concord some time ago now, and both the passengers and stage crew, ready for the southern run, were showing signs of impatience.

Standing together on the landing where they'd been talking for several minutes, Ben Charron and passen-

148

ger Doc Christian appeared oblivious to either sched-ules or impatient glances. Equally unaware of their surroundings were the young lovers whom Charron had just farewelled, now seated snugly side by side in the corner of the coach, facing the horses, as they waited for Christian to join them.

Nothing, it seemed, could intrude on the bliss of Ethan Clay and Felicity, both of whom, like so many in Capital City that overcast morning ten days later, were still a little dazed by the sequence of dramatic events following on directly from the wildest night in the Territory's history.

The elections had gone off with a whimper rather than a bang and the Republicans were installed for a second term, but without Governor Matherson Lane at their head. He had been forced to resign when allegations concerning his possible involvement in the by now noto-rious Ethan Clay affair had made his position untenable.

The judicial hearing into that case had been high-lighted dramatically when Judge Omar Burlinson – now referred to as 'The Singing Judge' in the *Territory News* – stood up in the dock before his peers on the bench and admitted having been coerced into know-ingly bringing down a guilty verdict against an inno-cent man, Ethan Clay, in order to assist Lane's re-elec-tion ambitions.

Clay was subsequently set free, even though he freely admitted that he'd been involved in the horse-thieving raid on the Valdez spread the night the rich man was slain. It had become increasingly apparent

149

throughout the long, hot days in the courthouse that Clay, although certainly no cleanskin, had been more the victim than the perpetrator in the saga which almost cost him his life. He was revealed as a victim of his own fame, the finest horseman in the Territory. It was this which had elevated him to the position of figurehead for the Red Creek Gang, even though a close examination of his involvement revealed him clearly as far more of a wild boy than a criminal like his companions.

While Strat Dalton was dismissed from office and released on a bond pending wider investigations into his alleged wrongdoing, the two surviving Red Creek boys, the Garcia brothers, each fetched twenty years in Territory.

Authorities were understandably eager to catch and try Harlan Jenner as soon as possible, but it was generally conceded that the killer would prove difficult, if not impossible, to track down.

It was understood that some sort of 'arrangement' between the courts and Clay had been reached whereby the latter might expect to live free if he mended his ways, on the proviso that he not pursue the territorial judicial system for damages through the Federal courts.

A gust of wind with a real chill on its breath buffeted the two men up on the landing. The muffled driver stamped his boots against the splashboard both to maintain circulation and to remind someone that it was time to go.

150

'You'd better get on board if you're going,' Charron said after a silence. Conversation was proving difficult. The two had proven, once again, to be a unique fighting team, but in reality neither man was really the team type.

'You're still denying reality, you fool!' The aftermath of all the heady drama and excitement had seen the Doc return to his tetchy, testy ways. He had a flask in his hip pocket and a cigarette jutted from between his teeth.

'Dammit! Can't you see? This is the start of your new life. So why the hell aren't you taking this stage south with us?'

Charron's manner was vague as he looked across at the stage. Clay and Felicity waved like he was their dearest friend. Their farewells had been warm, even touching, for from the moment he'd realized Clay was innocent, Charron had thrown his full weight behind securing the man's full acquittal and release. What their future might become he had no notion. But when you were young and in love, things had a way of working out, he knew that much.

'Talk sense, man,' he growled. 'Why would I want to go south? I'm going hunting Jenner.'

'You know you're not. Why lie?'

'Better make yourself plain, mister. It seems to me you've been acting like someone nursing a big secret ever since the night we closed down the city. It's not like you to clam up, you being such a world champion talker, that is.'

'All right. For her, I will.'

'Don't start about Terasina—'

'You're through,' Christian snapped.

Rain-coloured eyes turned chill. 'What?'

'Come on, unbend for once in your life.' Christian hefted his valise. 'We both know your great crusade is over. I saw you burn out on riot night when you couldn't fire a shot. But I already knew you were through even before that. It was in your eyes after you brought Clay in and when you faced Jenner. You had him cold, but couldn't finish him. In Abilene, you were a zealot who wanted to erase every killer, train-jumper, cow thief and crooked politico in the West. You were obsessive in a way that drove me crazy, Terasina too. But now all that's gone and you should be a happy man. Free. Only you're not, are you?'

'I've got to find Jenner.'

'He'll kill you if you do.'

'I'm a hard man to kill.'

Doc was disgusted, yet surprisingly patient for a rare moment.

'Charron, this is me. I'm the man that's seen it all. I've been a gun and been around guns all my life because I love the life. I'm a natural-born shootist, like Hickok or Earp. We never burn out because gunplay and killing come natural to us. But it never was for you. You were forced to become a shootist the day you took on a commitment to dead war heroes. And nobody ever did it better. But it was never you. And it had to come apart. Suddenly you'd seen too many ghosts, had

152

one too many bad dreams, heard one too many death rattles. Now you're through. But don't look at it that way. You've given fifteen years of your lousy life to a cause. Let others tote the load. You're free, goddamnit – free! Trust me, I'm the doctor.'

'*Adios*, Doc.'

'What about Terasina? What do I tell her?'

But the big man was already walking away. A red-faced Doc Christian flipped his butt away and tramped across to the coach, his coat tails flapping.

'Still thinks he's playing God!' he muttered, climbing in and thumbing a big heavy man out of the corner seat he'd selected for himself. He sat and scowled. 'Why was I fool enough to think that a man like him might have changed? That he could? Well, he'll get himself killed if he goes on believing he's that kind of creation. So let him. Who cares?'

His fellow passengers studied him as the horses hit their harness straps and the big muddy Concord lurched fowards – the young couple with alarm, the others warily. Then the heavy man felt confident enough to remark, 'Guess you hate him too, huh, Mr Christian? Lots of folks do, even if he did a power of good—'

'Hate him?' Doc Christian flared. 'Are you crazy, you fat shoat? That man's got more character in his little finger than all you gutless nothings who aren't fit to shine his boots put together!'

He hauled his flask from his hip pocket and unscrewed the cap. They watched in silence as he took

153

a slug then turned his head to scowl out the window at the last of the adobes sliding by. Nobody understood Doc Christian, not even Ethan Clay, whose life he'd helped save, nor the pretty girl at his side. But that was OK. Doc didn't understand himself either.

A chill, needle-like drizzle was falling across the winter prairies as the big man in a travel-stained slicker rode slowly along the muddy Minnesota road towards the next town.

Winter had come early to the north country, but Charron didn't seem to notice. Jenner's flimsy trail had led him from Colorado through Nebraska and into the Dakotas, Rapid City, Fargo, then across the line into Minnesota where, somewhere between Hoganville and Fox River, it had finally petered out altogether. More miles than a man could tally and nothing but cold country ahead, yet Charron held to the trail like a man for whom there was no letting go.

In the timber town of Belltree there wasn't even any paper on Jenner, despite Southwest Territory having a thousand-dollar warrant on his head. So Charron got back on his horse and pushed for the one-horse Chisolm, whose sole claim to importance was that the single track of the Northwest Railroad ran through it.

He'd decided to take a train to Illinois where Jenner was reported to have holed up once. That was all he had to go on – a big state and one trailwise outlaw who hadn't been sighted in – how long now? Close to four months. What were the odds? A million-to-one?

If Ethan Clay Should Hang

Chisolm comprised a quarter-mile front street cut three times by cross streets that went nowhere, surely the bleakest and most lonesome outpost this far-travelling man had seen since quitting Capital City.

He checked his horse at the livery and made his weary way through the mud to the general store-cum-roomer. He was booking a room with the storekeeper, when he noticed the room in the back, where he could see a man standing behind a rough bar. 'We also serve liquor here, mister,' the man smiled. 'You look like you could use a drink.'

He was lighting up a Dollar cheroot as he ducked his head below the low doorway. Two men stood leaning against the rough plank bar, a nondescript fellow in miner's Levi's and a tall man in a black shirt sporting twin tied-down holsters that seemed oddly out of place in backwoods Minnesota.

Maybe it was because he was so played out that he barely spared the drinkers a glance, or it could have been because the trail had gone stone-cold and Chisolm was such a nothing town that he was looking only for the barkeep. But then the tall drinker turned his head and Charron was staring into the handsome, but murderous face of Harlan Jenner.

'You!' the gunslinger hissed, and instantly launched into his magical sweeping draw that saw both guns clear leather even before Charron's dead Vesta hit the boards.

Charron lunged at him. It wasn't a premeditated action. Until that moment he'd had no notion of how he would react to a life or death situation. Now he was in one – and still could not use his guns!

The killer's black eyes opened wide in disbelief. Then he grinned wolfishly, as nickel-plated pistols reached firing level, barely able to believe his luck. Charron saw the knuckle of his forefinger whiten as he squeezed the trigger. He twisted his body violently as gunflame blossomed and he felt a hot knife of pain in his side, the brutal impact of the bullet almost driving him off balance, but not quite.

His driving shoulder caught the gunman squarely in the chest. The gun exploded again and the slug slammed harmlessly into the earth between his boots. Charron's left hook crunched home to the jaw and drove the killer back into the solid bar with such force that the entire structure collapsed under impact. Blood spilled hot and crimson from Jenner's broken mouth as he sagged drunkenly, directly into a second blow that felled him like a dead man.

Barman, customer and storekeeper waited in frozen silence for what might come next. But it was all over. All the big stranger did was press his hand against his side and stare absently at the blood oozing through his fingers. Another two inches to the right and it would have been him down on the dirty floor, dying.

And in that moment he finally understood and believed what Doc Christian had told him months earlier. It truly was all over. But he'd had to find out for certain, and now he knew he'd never use a gun again. And, dammit, Doc was right again when he'd talked about freedom. For, even though he was in pain and bleeding profusely, that was how he felt – free. The strange odyssey of commitment to an ideal, which had begun in a blood-drenched cornfield in Tennessee all that time ago and consumed him for so long, was truly over. He could accept now that his whole life had changed forever, that he was no longer a 'crusader' but simply a man, alone without friends, fortune or a future – yet he had never felt so fine in fifteen years. Free at last!

Then he sat down before he fell, and calmly told the drinker and the storekeeper what to do.

They hanged Harlan Jenner on the gallows built for Ethan Clay the same week in which the killer's testimony saw Strat Dalton draw twenty years in Territory.

Ben Charron did not appear at Capital City during the trials or later. In the year that followed, he was more than ever a man alone who now traded horses and occasionally guided a wagon train to some place folks wanted to go. He scouted for the Army on several occasions, and once did a stint for the law in Tucson, tracking for a posse hunting a band of killers. They caught their quarry, but he took no part in the showdown. He no longer even carried a gun.

Arizona, Nevada, New Mexico, Sonora and Texas – all saw the big-shouldered rider in brown astride the mouse-blue horse that summer, winter and fall. Saw him, recognized him, whispered about what he'd once been and were rarely sorry to see him ride on, not for what he was now, but because they remembered what he'd been back then.

Until one lonesome night with storm clouds threatening saw the man ride alone into San Diablo, just another border town where folks were no better or worse than any place else, where the mayor was as corrupt as Judas and the Cowgirl Palace was no different from a thousand saloons from Waco to Tucson – but at least it boasted some decent rooming-houses. So the big brown man with fifty hard miles behind him immediately set out in the thunderstorm, which struck with theatrical fury, great bomb blasts of thunder and jagged lightning, the bolts seemingly bent on striking him down in his tracks as he tramped the muddy streets.

The chill rain was refreshing, yet he felt he was walking like an old man as he crossed at an intersection and continued on. The building on his right looked much like the others except for the fact that the occupants had already lit all the lamps when the storm brought dusk an hour ahead of time, lending it a bright and welcoming look. He paused, then noticed the sign erected on the gallery roof between the gabled windows.

Welcome To Terasina's.

He stared, standing there in the soaking rain shaking his head, astonished that something as simple as a name could come like a hit to the heart.

Then, like someone in the grip of something stronger than himself, he mounted the steps. Through the streaming panes of a large window, he caught a glimpse of a tall figure in grey moving briskly about laying places at a table. And something in the way the woman moved jolted him back to Abilene and he thought, 'No, it couldn't be . . . but then maybe . . .'

He went in.

Standing dripping in the brightly lit bay window of the supper room, with two young maids regarding him curiously from the desk, he watched the woman complete the table she was working on, already knowing it was her.

He knew he should turn and leave. All he'd ever brought her was pain, and he'd vowed never to do so again. Then the woman straightened abruptly as though sensing a presence. She whirled round sharply and he was staring into Terasina's dark eyes once again and astonishingly felt his vision begin to blur.

'Ben!'

Her voice reached him from across the gulf of time. There was a beat like that of great slow wings in his head as he stood waiting for her contempt and rejection. He knew he deserved both, and yet in his heart he knew that he'd kept her out of his bloody life not because he didn't love her, but because he *did*.

He found he couldn't move, but no such inhibitions shackled Terasina Moreno. She was coming towards him almost as though she'd been expecting him, moving with that remembered quick grace, dark eyes never leaving his for a moment.

'Terasina—'

'No, do not say anything, *hombrecito*.' She reached out and took his hands. 'There is no need. I've been expecting you, don't you see?'

He blinked. He couldn't be hearing right. How could she have ever expected him again? It was over two years . . .

'How? Why?' he managed to say.

'Why, Doc of course. He told me to be patient, but to expect you someday. He told me you'd been freed of your burden, and swore you would come find me, *caballero*, even made me believe it. Indeed, he was so certain of this that he finally gave up carrying a torch for me and married a rich widow from Kansas. In his wedding speech he said he owed his new happiness to you – and he was not even being sarcastic, for once.'

'That Doc . . .'

She squeezed his hands tightly. There were tears in her eyes.

'I understand everything, Benjamin. You are at last home from the war. Welcome home, *mi caballero*.'

The wind hurled the deluge even more furiously against the streaming glass of the big bay windows as he drew her into his arms, but for Ben Charron and Terasina Moreno it was the gentlest rain that ever fell.